DUST DEVIL
DALTON SAVAGE
BOOK 6

L.T. RYAN

WITH
BIBA PEARCE

Copyright © 2025 by L.T. Ryan, Biba Pearce, Brian Christopher Shea, & Liquid Mind Media. All rights reserved. No part of this publication may be copied, reproduced in any format, by any means, electronic or otherwise, without prior consent from the copyright owner and publisher of this book. This is a work of fiction. All characters, names, places and events are the product of the author's imagination or used fictitiously.

For information contact:

contact@ltryan.com

http://LTRyan.com

https://www.facebook.com/groups/1727449564174357

THE DALTON SAVAGE SERIES

Savage Grounds

Scorched Earth

Cold Sky

The Frost Killer

Crimson Moon

Dust Devil

Savage Season

Join the L.T. Ryan reader family & receive a free copy of the Rachel Hatch story, *Fractured*. Click the link below to get started:

https://ltryan.com/rachel-hatch-newsletter-signup-1

ONE

SHERIFF DALTON SAVAGE pulled off the main road, his black Chevy Suburban spitting gravel as it crunched onto the cracked lakebed. The air was dry as a bone, the kind of heat that made you sweat from the inside out. Even with the window down, all he could smell was dust.

The reservoir had been low for years, but last week the bottom finally gave up its last muddy secrets. Now it was just dry, sun-bleached earth, and in the middle of it, ringed off with crime scene tape that fluttered in the warm breeze, were a pile of bones.

He killed the engine and stepped out. His boots cracked the crusty top layer of soil, sinking into the damper one underneath, a reminder that this ground hadn't been walked on in a long time.

Deputy Sinclair was already there. She stood near the perimeter, arms folded, Ray-Bans reflecting the crime scene. Her hand rested on her hip, just inches from her Glock.

"Morning, Sheriff," she said, nodding once. "You're not going to like this one."

Savage adjusted his belt, the radio at his side squawking briefly before he silenced it. "I don't like any of them."

They walked together toward the remains. The bones were sprawled awkwardly in the dirt. Pale ribs splayed open like a broken fan, the skull tilted sideways as if the man had tried to turn away from whatever was coming. Tattered denim clung to the skeleton's legs, weather-worn and stiff. A cracked leather boot was still laced on one foot.

"Local kids found it while they were out messing around with dirt bikes," Sinclair said. "They came across the boot, then saw the rest."

"What's that?" He squinted down at what appeared to be a strip of worn leather next to the body.

"Not sure. Could've been a leather satchel or bag of some sort."

Savage grunted, then crouched beside the remains. There wasn't much flesh left, just shreds of skin clinging to bone. A chain necklace still rested on the collarbone, a worn emblem hanging from it, scorched and blackened. It looked like an iron cross.

He glanced up. "Where's the other boot?"

Sinclair pointed. "Over there. About thirty feet east. Could've come loose after he was dumped in the lake, or due to the currents or shifting silt."

Savage stood and turned in a slow circle. Hawk's Landing shimmered in the distance, the rooftops blurring beyond the heat waves. They'd had a few quiet months since their last case. God knows they'd needed it. The Guardian Bear killings had resonated in the local press for weeks before finally dying down.

He hoped this discovery wouldn't stir it up again. The last thing this town—*his* town—needed was more bad publicity.

"Ray's on his way," Sinclair said. "He's bringing Pearl with him."

A quick nod. "Good."

Ray was the town's medical examiner. Originally from Denver, he and his wife, Pearl, a retired forensic specialist, had settled in Hawk's Landing a couple of years back. "We're looking forward to a quiet retirement," Ray had told him at their first crime scene.

How ironic that statement had turned out to be.

He often used them for local jobs, since it saved time and was more convenient and less expensive than calling out a team from Durango, the next big town. Hawk's Landing's Sheriff's Department wasn't awash with funds, unfortunately.

Ray and Pearl were a power duo. Reliable, experienced, and enterprising. Plus, they'd proved they could handle even the most complicated of investigations—and they'd seen a few.

Savage gazed down at the remains. "Looks like he's been here a while. Years, maybe."

Sinclair waved her hand around. "His body would have been lying at the bottom of the lake all this time, and nobody knew."

"Somebody knew."

Savage spotted an item tucked under the skeleton's right arm and took a step closer. It looked like a weathered piece of fabric. Using a pen, he slid it out from underneath the remains.

Not just fabric. A patch.

A biker's bottom rocker.

He could just make out the name of the club.

The Crimson Angels.

He gave a low whistle. "See this?"

Sinclair's eyebrows shot up when she realized what it was. "That will help us get an ID, or at the very least, narrow it down."

"It also gives us a place to start."

The sound of a car engine sputtering made them turn around. An ancient station wagon approached, kicking up a plume of dust in its wake.

"That's them." Sinclair nodded toward the car.

The battered Ford Taurus came to a halt and the middle-aged Ray climbed out. He waved, popped the hatch, and proceeded to pull on a Tyvek suit, mask and gloves. His wife Pearl, dressed casually in jeans, a loose-fitting shirt, and an enormous straw hat, walked over to them.

"I heard you found some remains. How old are we talking?" Her eyes gleamed with interest.

Savage grinned. To anyone else, they appeared to be just another retired couple, but he knew they both possessed razor sharp intellects and a professional fascination with the dead.

"I was hoping you'd be able to tell me."

Pearl walked over to the body, making sure she stayed out of the contamination zone. Focusing her gaze, she said, "Judging by the state of decomposition and the clothes, I'd say at least a couple of years, but Ray will be able to confirm."

Her husband, covered head to toe and ready to inspect the body, came over. "This used to be a lake, you say?"

Sinclair nodded. "Until recently, yeah. The drought has completely dried it out."

"Such a shame." Pearl surveyed the desolate landscape. "It'll affect the level of decomp."

Her husband grunted in agreement as he crouched down beside the remains. With steady hands, he inspected the rib cage, then the skull.

"What you got?" Savage was impatient to establish a timeline. Conflicts and violence were common in the outlaw motorcycle club, so it would help to have an idea of when this guy went missing.

Ray's eyes sharpened behind his mask. "I'd say he's been here for at least three to four years. I can't be more exact without doing a full autopsy."

Savage rubbed the perspiration from his forehead. He'd been hoping for something more definite than that.

Sinclair tilted her head to get a better look at what the man might have been wearing. "We might be able to date him by his clothes."

"I can tell you how he died, though," Ray added, a glint in his eye.

Savage turned his attention back to the ME. "Go ahead."

"Do you see the entry wound here? It's located in the center of the frontal bone, just above the eyebrows in the middle of the forehead."

Savage leaned in and stared at the disfigured skull. Time and exposure to the elements had left it misshapen and grotesque. "Yeah."

"He was shot with a 9mm Luger round."

Savage frowned. "How'd you know that?"

Ray chuckled. "The shape of the wound is circular, which typically indicates that the bullet entered at a straight angle. There is no exit wound, so the bullet didn't pass through the skull. It remained lodged inside the cranial cavity."

Savage widened his eyes. "It's still there?"

"Yep, it's trapped in the bone. If you look closely, you can see part of it through the fracture."

Ray reached down, inserted forceps between the skull fragments with practiced hands, and extracted a dark, compact slug. He held it up so they could see. "This was a classic close-range shot. The shooter got him right between the eyes."

Sinclair held out a forensic bag, and Ray dropped the bullet inside.

Savage tightened his jaw. "So, this was an execution."

TWO

SAVAGE PARKED his Suburban at the end of the quiet cul-de-sac, killing the headlights. The houses here were spaced wide apart, their porches set back from the road, with scrubby lots and low fences giving way to open fields. Behind the row of houses, the outline of the foothills loomed in the dark, sharp against the clear, moonlit sky.

No reason to advertise his presence. His SUV with the Sheriff's office decal on the side would draw unwanted attention, especially when it showed up outside the house of the President of the Crimson Angels MC late at night. People noticed those kinds of things.

The stars twinkled over the jagged mountain peaks as he hiked the last hundred yards through dry grass and low brush to her house.

It was risky coming here, but not as risky as turning up unannounced at Mac's Roadhouse, the biker bar on the Durango Road and the Crimson Angels' unofficial headquarters.

Given the late hour, and the fact that he'd driven past the Roadhouse and hadn't seen Rosalie's motorcycle out front, he guessed she was at home.

Rosalie Weston, self-proclaimed President of the Crimson

Angels, was a dangerous woman, but he'd rather tackle her alone than with her club behind her.

He took the long way around, staying low, boots quiet on the packed earth. The back porch was screened by sagebrush and a half-dead willow tree. He stepped around the side, one hand resting loosely near his sidearm, just in case. He was three steps from the porch when a voice snapped behind him.

"Turn around, real slow."

He did, raising his hands in the process.

Rosalie stood behind him, a Glock 19 leveled at his chest. Her hand was steady. When she saw his face, she exhaled sharply and lowered the gun.

"Jesus, Dalton. You scared the shit out of me."

He lowered his arms, giving her a half grin. "Didn't mean to startle you."

She tucked the gun into the back of her jeans and stepped forward into the porch light. Long, black hair flowed sleek and straight down her back, a smudgy green shirt clung to her slender frame, and her tanned arms glistened with lean muscle and biker tattoos. Despite the flowing hair and loose top, there was nothing soft about her. Rosalie was all sharp eyes and harder edges.

She shook her head at him. "You want to be careful sneaking up on people like that. Could get yourself shot."

"I'll try calling next time."

She snorted, then nodded for him to follow her inside.

They weren't friends, but they weren't enemies either. Associates, maybe? They used each other, when it suited them.

Rosalie had used him to run the Mexicans out of town when they tried to take over her drug distribution network some years back, and he'd used the club's collective prowess when Becca and his son had been kidnapped.

Since then, they had developed a grudging respect for each other, but she was still an outlaw, and he was still a lawman. Like oil and water, they didn't mix.

He stepped onto the porch behind her and went through the back door into the kitchen. A floral scent lingered briefly in her wake, but while sweet and alluring, it didn't soften her.

She glanced over her shoulder. "Why are you prowling around here anyway?"

"Didn't want the neighbors to talk."

She grabbed two glasses and a bottle of bourbon from the countertop and poured them each a finger. "My neighbors know better than to talk."

He grunted, preferring not to dwell on what that meant.

She handed him one of the tumblers. "But if anyone in the club finds out you were here, that's my fucking head on a block." She shot him a hard look before taking a sip.

"They won't." Savage leaned against the wall, holding the glass in his hand. The kitchen was neat and functional. No frills. No little nicknacks. Nothing personal. Typical Rosalie. "I parked out of sight and nobody saw me."

Her gaze roamed over his face, lingering on his chest, or was it the badge? Narrowing, they darted back to his face. "I take it this isn't a social call?"

He pushed away from the wall. "Unfortunately not. We found a body in the dried-up lake outside of town."

That got her attention. "A body?"

"What's left of it, yeah."

Jade-green eyes slanted at him. "Who is it?"

"I thought maybe you could tell me."

She stiffened. "How should I know?"

Savage set his glass on the countertop, its contents untouched. "We found a patch on him, Rosalie. A Crimson Angels patch. He was part of the club."

"A lot of men have worn that patch over the years," she said carefully.

"It would've been three or four years ago, possibly more. Back when Axle was President."

Her face didn't twitch, but her voice turned a few degrees colder. "Then ask him."

"I intend to, but I thought I'd come to you first. See if you remember anyone who went missing around then. This guy had an iron cross pendant on a silver chain around his neck."

Rosalie studied her glass. "Doesn't ring any bells."

Savage tapped his forehead with his finger. "He was shot in the head, then his body was dumped in the lake. Ringing any bells now?"

She lifted her gaze, steady and defiant. "Sorry, Dalton. I can't help you."

He studied her. Tight-lipped and tense, she was holding back. "Can't or won't?"

She sighed. "Look, I don't know what happened, okay? I wasn't involved in club business back then. Axle kept me locked out."

Savage snorted. "You ran the club, even then. Axle just didn't know it yet."

She smirked. "That may be, but I didn't have anything to do with the day-to-day shit, if you get my drift. If someone had a beef with another member, they took care of it. I wasn't privy to that."

Her witchy eyes held him. She was good. Probably the best liar he'd ever seen—and he'd seen a few—but he had no doubt she was bullshitting. Not much happened in the club, then or now, that Rosalie didn't know about.

She picked up her drink again. "My advice, Dalton, is to leave this one alone. Feuds happen. Sometimes people disappear. It's the way of the life."

He frowned. "You're saying this was club business?"

"I'm saying club loyalty runs deeper than blood. You're either in or you're out. There's no in between."

His gaze locked with hers. "Give me a name, Rosalie."

She didn't answer, just looked out the window toward the dark shadow of the mountains.

"Rosalie?" he prompted.

A shrug. "I can't. I don't know who it is."

A long beat passed.

She downed the remainder of her drink.

Eventually, he said, "You could find out."

The glass hit the countertop. "Jesus, Dalton. You want to get me kicked out of my own club?"

"I just mean to ask around. Scooter might remember, or one of the other guys."

"You don't think that's suspicious, me suddenly asking questions about someone who disappeared over three years ago?"

"Not if you play it right."

She sighed, calming down. "If I wasn't told, it was because whoever shot him wanted to keep it quiet. Asking questions is going to rip open that wound again."

"Only if the murderer is still in the club."

She frowned. "You think it was Axle?"

He raked a hand through his hair, frustrated. "I don't know who it was. I don't even know who the victim is."

She put her hands on her hips and glared at him. "Well, I can't just bring it up."

He thought for a moment. "You want me and my deputies to come over to the Roadhouse? Stir up some shit?"

She rolled her eyes. "Not really, but it might help. At least that would give me a reason to bring it up."

"Fine, I can do that. Tomorrow afternoon suit you?"

She gave a curt nod. "Fine. Now, are you going to drink that or stare at it for the rest of the night? I want you off my property before someone sees you."

He downed it in one, then turned and pulled open the screen that covered the back door. "Good seeing you, Rosalie."

"Wish I could say the same, Sheriff."

THREE

THE CEILING FAN in the squadroom was doing a poor job pretending it worked. It spun lazily overhead, pushing the warm air around in circles. Savage stood in front of his team, one hand braced against the whiteboard, the other wrapped around a paper cup of black coffee. The air conditioning had given up around ten a.m., and Barbara, their administrative assistant and office gatekeeper, was on the phone with the county maintenance crew for the third time that morning.

Outside, it was even hotter. The scrubland surrounding the town was dry and cracked, while the reservoir had dropped another inch overnight. Brushfires had started crawling down from the northern ridgelines, smoke seeping into the valley air. The whole town smelled like scorched weeds and dry pine.

Savage cleared his throat. "All right, listen up."

Sinclair swung away from her monitor. Thorpe leaned back in his chair, boots crossed at the ankles. Lucas McBride, their latest recruit, stood at the back. He'd been a deputy for almost two months already and was fitting in well. It helped that he used to be a U.S. Marine and knew how to handle himself, unlike Littleton, his predecessor, who'd never really come to grips with the more active side of the job.

Lucas had a rugged, tanned face, a square jaw, and close-cut hair. His forearms were crisscrossed with scars and tattoos, but there was a quiet intensity behind his eyes. The kind of guy who watched more than he spoke.

"Earlier this morning, Sinclair and I were called to the scene of a body found in the dried-up lakebed. According to the ME, the victim had been there for some time."

"At least three years," Sinclair added.

Savage nodded and pinned up the photographs Pearl had taken at the crime scene. The first was an aerial shot of the lakebed, showing the yellow tape and the skeletal outline barely visible in the dirt.

"Is that a drone shot?" Thorpe, their resident technical whiz, asked.

"Yeah, Pearl's new toy. It's pretty cool," Sinclair told him. "Gives us a bird's eye view of the whole area."

Thorpe crossed his arms. "Impressive."

Savage pinned up a photograph of the remains, including the worn denim jeans, what was left of the leather jacket, and the bones stripped clean by fish other lake creatures. The team fell silent. Even Barb stopped typing in the background.

"Meet our victim. Male, Caucasian, judging by the bone structure, early thirties."

They all stared at the grim photographs.

Savage continued. "As Sinclair said, estimated time of death was around three years ago. According to Ray, he was killed by a single gunshot wound to the head—9mm. We recovered the slug at the scene."

Lucas spoke up. "Executed?"

Savage gave a tight nod. "Looks like it. As of yet, we have no ID on him."

"I'll search the Missing Persons database," Thorpe offered.

Savage pinned up the final photograph. "This was found under his body, probably fell off of his jacket. It's a biker patch."

Thorpe tilted his head to read the faded writing on the fabric, then he exhaled noisily. "Oh, boy."

"Yep, Crimson Angels," Sinclair confirmed.

"Is that significant?" Lucas glanced between them.

"The Crimson Angels are an outlaw motorcycle club led by a ruthless bi—, er, woman called Rosalie Weston." Sinclair had had her own share of run-ins with Rosalie over the years.

"A woman?" Lucas quirked an eyebrow. "Isn't that unusual?"

"Times are changing," Sinclair said, an edge to her voice.

"No offense. It's just that I didn't think 1%ers allowed women in their clubs," Lucas was quick to add.

"It would be a mistake to underestimate her," Savage warned, giving a wry smile. He ought to know. He'd done just that and suffered the consequences. She'd played him once, but he wouldn't make that mistake again.

"Think of it as a hostile takeover," Thorpe told him. "Emphasis on hostile."

"Got it." Lucas nodded.

"Maybe Rosalie knows who the victim is?" suggested Thorpe.

"I already spoke with her," Savage admitted, earning himself surprised glances from the rest of the team. Not even Sinclair knew he'd paid Rosalie a visit late last night.

"You did?" Her eyebrow quirked.

"Yeah, took the opportunity to catch her alone at her place on my way home." He didn't miss the look Sinclair shared with Thorpe. His relationship with Rosalie had always been tenuous. Even he didn't understand it fully.

They had a connection, sure. A mutual agreement, unspoken, of course. He might even respect her—just a little. It took guts to do what she did, even if she was on the other side of the law. He didn't condone the club's illegal activities, but he admired Rosalie's tenacity.

"What did she say?" Lucas asked, picking up on the others' surprise.

He shrugged. "Not much. Claimed she didn't know who the victim was and hadn't been privy to club business back then."

"Could be true." Sinclair shrugged. "Axle was president, and he didn't want her involved."

"Axle being—?" Lucas asked.

"Her ex-husband," Savage supplied. "And predecessor."

"Okay," he said, drawing out the "o."

"Like I said, ruthless." Sinclair punctuated that with a nod.

"She's doing a better job running the club than her husband ever did," Savage allowed. "At least she cooperates with us."

"Only when it serves her purpose," Sinclair added dryly.

He acknowledged that with a tilt of his head. "That's why we have to make sure it does."

Sinclair frowned. "I know that look. What did you have in mind?"

He grinned. "We're going to pay the Roadhouse a visit this afternoon. Stir things up a little."

"Seriously?" Sinclair's eyebrows shot up.

"The Roadhouse is—?" Lucas glanced at them.

"A biker bar on the Durango Road," Thorpe supplied. "Rough as hell. It's also the Crimson Angels' unofficial clubhouse. Rosalie owns the place."

"Gotcha."

"She's expecting us," Savage added.

"What's the point of the visit?" Lucas asked. He was astute. That was another thing Savage liked about him.

"Get the conversation going. We ask about the dead guy, leave a photo of his patch in the bar, get them talking about it. That way Rosalie's got an excuse to gather some intel for us."

Lucas slanted his gaze. "She's your C.I.?"

That made Savage chuckle. The thought of Rosalie as anyone's snitch was laughable. She only ever served her own self-interest. "Nope, but if she hears anything, I'm hoping she'll throw it my way."

"How does that benefit her?" Lucas asked.

"Because the murder might have something to do with her ex, who's serving time at Fremont for assault, attempted murder and bank robbery. If he—or any of his guys—were behind it, they go down, and she gets rid of the club members who don't like taking orders from a woman."

Lucas pursed his lips. "I'm beginning to see how this works."

"What about DNA or dental records?" Thorpe asked, steering them back to the victim.

"Pearl's on it," Savage confirmed with a nod. "She'll need a couple of days to get back to us, though."

Sinclair's phone beeped. She glanced down and frowned.

"What is it?" Thorpe asked.

"Mason says fires are creeping through the forest line north of Route 8. That's half a mile from the southern grazing perimeter. He's already short-staffed. The whole valley's bone-dry. If it spreads, we could be looking at evacuations by the weekend."

Savage gave a tight nod. "Let Mason know we'll assist if it comes to that. Meanwhile, let's concentrate on our vic. I want full background checks on anyone affiliated with the Crimson Angels between three and five years ago. Active members, prospects, associates. Most of them have rap sheets, so they shouldn't be too hard to find."

The team nodded.

"Then, we'll head out to the Roadhouse around two-thirty. Make some noise."

Lucas grinned. "Sounds like fun."

THE ROADHOUSE WAS A WEATHERED, low-lying building with a faded exterior. Savage, followed by Sinclair's police cruiser, pulled into the parking lot, kicking up dust as they came to a halt alongside a line of gleaming Harley-Davidsons.

The neon sign outside the bar was not flashing and looked tacky in the bright sunlight, while the sloping iron roof was tinged with rust.

There were at least half a dozen motorcycles parked out front. Chrome glinted, handlebars wrapped in black leather, tanks airbrushed with flames, skulls, and the red-winged insignia of the Crimson Angels.

Savage climbed out first, followed by Sinclair and Lucas. The temperature had peaked somewhere north of ninety, and the wind carried the scorched scent of burned vegetation and dry dirt. A dust devil swirled briefly across the lot before collapsing near a rusted-out pickup shell.

"Ready?" he asked.

Sinclair wiped her sunglasses on her shirt, then nodded.

Lucas scanned the line of bikes, the smudged windows, the rickety porch. He kept his right hand close to his belt—not on his gun, but near enough that any watchful eyes inside would take note. "Yeah."

"Let's go," Savage said and strode toward the front door.

The inside of the Roadhouse looked far less welcoming in the harsh light of day and smelled of beer mixed with the faint tinge of motor oil. Sunlight slanted through the windows, pooling on the scuffed wooden floors. Ceiling fans churned overhead, but the effect was minimal. The jukebox in the corner pumped out an old-school rock song, its bass thumping through the building.

Savage scanned the room, hand on his holster. A group of bikers sat at a scarred table with mismatched stools, talking and laughing. They fell silent when Savage and his team walked in. It wasn't often they were paid a visit by the Sheriff and his deputies.

Two other men played a game of pool at a table in the far corner, but they stopped, a ball ricocheting off the side and coming to a stop inches from the corner pocket.

Behind the bar stood one of the newest club members, Joel. He was in his mid-twenties, with a mop of unruly dark hair, and hard, unflinching eyes that spoke of a checkered past.

"Hey, Joel," Savage called to him. "Rosalie around?"

"She's busy," he quipped. Standard response. Rosalie would be checking them out from the secret cameras in the bar and would come out from the back office when she was good and ready.

A chair scraped. "You're not welcome here," a thick-set man in his forties with arms like beer kegs and a gut to match growled. His T-shirt was stretched tight across his chest. On top of it, he wore a sleeveless leather jacket with the Crimson Angels logo on it.

"I'll be the judge of that." Savage reached into his jacket pocket. Immediately four out of the five at the table went for their weapons.

"Whoa!" Lucas drew in response. Sinclair did the same, but she wasn't as fast. Savage appreciated the steadiness of Lucas's arm considering he had four guns pointed at him.

"Now, there's no need for that." Savage spread his arms wide so they could see them. In his hand was a crime scene photograph. "I just wanted to know whether any of you can identify this guy? He's one of you, or rather, he used to be."

Slowly, he stepped forward and laid the photograph on the table. After a few seconds, the bikers holstered their weapons.

Rosalie chose that moment to walk into the room. Dressed in no-nonsense black skinny jeans, lethal biker boots, and an uncompromising, figure-hugging top, she looked every inch the woman in charge. With her hair draped over one shoulder, harsh eye make-up, and a menacing smile on her lips, she cut a striking figure. Savage saw Lucas's eyes widen.

Rosalie had that effect on most men.

"Afternoon, ma'am." He dipped his head.

She stalked over to the table without greeting him in response. "What's this?"

Savage pointed to the photograph. "We're looking to ID that man."

She picked it up, studied it, then dropped it again. "I ain't seen him."

"Not asking if you've seen him, ma'am," Lucas interjected. "Asking if you know who he is."

She turned to study the newest deputy, green eyes flashing in the dim light. "Sorry, still can't help you."

Savage looked around the table at the five big bikers wearing patched jackets. "What about you guys?"

He got a grunt, a shake of the head, and three scowls.

Savage pursed his lips and gave a slow nod. "Take it that's a no, then?"

Sinclair stood at the door, still holding her weapon, just in case things kicked off. They had been known to go to hell in a handbasket pretty quickly in this bar.

"You done?" Rosalie asked, hands on snaky hips.

"Guess so." Savage gestured for Lucas to leave, then he nodded to the photograph. "I'll leave that here to jog your memories. If any of you remembers who he is, you know where to find me."

Sinclair turned and they followed her out of the door.

As they walked toward their vehicles, Savage let out a relieved breath. "I think that went well, all things considered."

FOUR

"DON'T FORGET you've got a function at Councilman Royce Beckett's home tonight," Barb reminded him when they got back to the Sheriff's office.

Damn. He'd forgotten all about that.

His chest constricted. If only Becca were here to accompany him. She was good at shmoozing and talking shop. He was terrible at it.

He sighed.

Except she wasn't here. Not anymore.

After he'd told her he was running for a second term, she'd sat him down and explained why she couldn't be with him any longer. As torn up as he was, he'd half expected it. Things between them hadn't been right for a while now—not since she'd lied to him about knowing a suspect in his last case.

He understood why she'd done it—of course he did—but to think she had a secret past he didn't know about. A life she'd said nothing about. That Becca wasn't even her real name, for God's sake. It felt like a betrayal.

So, when she'd said she was leaving, he hadn't protested too much.

"Don't even think about cancelling," Barb warned him, following him into his office. "You didn't go to the last one, and this office needs his support."

"Yeah, I know," he grumbled, unfastening his hostler and laying it on his desk.

"We need new radios," Barb reminded him, standing just inside the door. "Half the squad's still using analog units from a decade ago and they cut out every time we hit the canyon roads."

Savage dropped into his chair with a grunt. "I put in that request three months ago."

"And it's sitting in limbo with the county budget committee, which Beckett chairs." She crossed her arms. "We need the digital comms and the wildfire inter-op funding, so you'd better go to that party."

Savage pinched the bridge of his nose. "Is that all?"

She gave him a sharp look. "Nope. Now that you mention it, we could do with new tires for the cruisers and a proper tech upgrade for Thorpe."

"He's already reminded me of that."

Barb nodded but didn't stop talking. "And I know this isn't high up on your priority list, but the detention cells need a full inspection before the state audit next quarter. If we fail, the whole department could be shut down."

Savage exhaled and stared out the window for a long beat. Beyond the glass, the heat haze warped the edge of the courthouse. Somewhere out in the hills, smoke was still rising. He wondered how Mason and his crew of firefighters were getting on.

"I know," he said, turning back to her. "Don't worry. I'll go. Smile, shake hands, talk about grant requests and procurement plans. Anything else?"

Barb smiled faintly. "Yeah. Try not to punch anybody."

He grimaced. "That, I can't promise."

. . .

SAVAGE ARRIVED at Councilman Royce Beckett's house just before sunset. Situated south of Hawk's Landing, near the Southern Ute reservation and newly built casino complex, the place was a sprawling mansion laid out over a couple of acres. He admired the white stucco walls and red-tile roof of the main house while he drove up a curved driveway long enough to land a small plane.

Leaving his SUV out front, he stepped under an archway adorned with string lights glowing softly in the twilight. The only blemish on the ambience was the smell of smoke hovering above the town. He couldn't deny it created a spectacular sunset, but it also deepened the growing unease sparked by the wildfires.

The front door was open, and he tugged at the collar of his shirt as he stepped inside. The tie felt like a noose. He hated political games. Hated small talk, posturing, and glad-handing. It wasn't that he couldn't play the game, he just had no stomach for the kind of men who did. As sheriff, he'd sworn to protect the people of Hawk's Landing—not brown nose the ones who thought they ran it.

But Barb was right. The radios, the IT funding, the holding cells, they all hinged on Beckett's goodwill, and in a town like this, goodwill was as transactional as a bar tab. Part of his job was to get them what they needed.

"They're out back, sir," a server in a black polo shirt told him, as she stopped to offer him a glass of sparkling wine on a silver tray.

Shaking his head to the drink, he proceeded through a vast entrance hall and out into a courtyard, where the cocktail party was already in full swing. A string quartet played from an upper balcony, while well-dressed men and glamorous women sipped imported wines and mingled, talking shop.

Beckett spotted him and strode over, arms outstretched. "Sheriff Savage. This is a pleasant surprise."

Savage offered a tight smile and shook the man's hand. "Good evening, Councilman."

Beckett wore a cream linen blazer, no tie, and held a drink in his left hand. His salt-and-pepper hair was trimmed to perfection, and he sported a well-entrenched golfer's tan.

"Isn't it? Glad you could make it." Beckett steered him toward the bar. "I was beginning to think you didn't like us."

"Been busy."

"Of course. Of course. I heard about your body in the lakebed."

Savage glanced at him but said nothing.

"Got any leads?" Beckett prompted.

"Not yet. We're waiting on an ID." Savage did not want to go into that tonight. He had other matters to discuss. There was nothing to tell, anyway.

"Mayor's around here somewhere," Beckett continued. "And a few of your friends from downtown. Come on, I'll walk with you."

Savage followed him into the main reception room, cool with air conditioning and smelling faintly of cologne and cigars. The ceiling soared above them, beams exposed, modern art on the walls. A stone fireplace big enough to roast a deer caught his eye, with neat stacks of wood placed in racks to one side.

Jasper McAllister, the mayor of Hawk's Landing, held court in a corner with a glass of bourbon in hand, laughing at something John Littleton had just said.

McAllister turned as he spotted him. "Sheriff."

He stepped forward with a politician's polish and clapped a hand on Savage's shoulder. "Good to see you. Congratulations again on your re-election."

"Thanks for your endorsement." Savage shook the mayor's hand. It had been over two months since he'd taken the pledge to serve Hawk's Landing for another term.

Two months since Becca had left, taking Connor with her.

John Littleton scowled at him. Tall, tanned, and with the physique of a lumberjack despite being in his late fifties, he ran a successful logging business. Actually, make that the most successful logging business in the county. Wealthy, well connected, and with a family history stretching back to the founding fathers, John Littleton was a force to be reckoned with. They'd had a few run-ins in the past.

"Sheriff." Littleton inclined his head.

"How's Kevin doing, John?" Savage dispensed with the small talk. He didn't like his former deputy's father. Just because he had money and power, he thought he could run roughshod over everybody else, including his own son.

Littleton shrugged. "Seems happy enough, no thanks to you."

Savage hadn't wanted to fire the kid, but he'd had no choice. Kevin had withheld information in order to protect his uncle, Sam Littleton, a suspect in a murder investigation. It would be a chargeable offense for a civilian, but for a deputy, it was downright unacceptable.

No thanks to you either, he thought.

McAllister grinned. "Don't mind him, Sheriff. You did what you had to do."

"Kevin never had the stomach for the job," Littleton griped, his mouth set in a firm line.

Savage gave a small nod, not rising to the bait.

Bob Cullen came from across the room. Older now, a little slower, but still sharp as hell. He owned the general store and knew more about what went on in Hawk's Landing than any of the suits.

"Dalton." Bob gripped his hand firmly. "I was hoping to see you tonight."

"Bob," Savage said, his expression warming. He liked the old guy. "How's things?"

"Dry," Bob said simply. "We need some goddamn rain. My suppliers are charging double for anything fresh, and I'm having trouble stocking bottled water."

"Sorry to hear that." The drought was affecting everyone.

"No sign of rain anytime soon," McAllister said with a grimace.

That was the problem. Savage thought of Mason and his team, fighting to contain the brush fires so they wouldn't turn lethal, and the suits in here, wining and dining and pampering each other's egos.

Beckett reappeared beside them. "Let me know if there's anything I can do to help, Bob."

"Thanks." Bob nodded.

This was his moment. Savage turned to Beckett. "Any news on those radios we asked for?"

Beckett smiled like a man who knew when he held the power. "I'll look into that for you, Dalton. Give the committee a push."

Savage held back his irritation. "Appreciate that. There are a few other areas that need attention too." He went on to ask about the other items on Barbara's list, reminding himself that they needed this. That it was for the good of the town. Hopefully, Beckett would see that.

Beckett nodded seriously, appearing to be concerned, but not enough to write anything down. Savage would have to chase up with a phone call during office hours.

Not wanting to disappear straight away, he forced himself to make small talk for a short while, before moving away to greet some other people he knew.

Eventually, however, he excused himself from the cluster and wandered out onto the lawn, hoping to escape the noise and the clink of glassware. He stood for a moment, hands in his pockets, looking out over the darkening foothills. Smoke from the mountain fires drifted along the horizon like the ghost of a storm.

His phone buzzed.

He answered it. "Savage."

Ray's voice came through, quiet but clear. "Got an ID for you, Sheriff."

Yes, finally.

He straightened. "Talk to me."

"Your victim is Diesel Vaughn. Real name is Dean Vaughn. Dental records are a match."

DUST DEVIL

Savage turned back to look at the party. The laughter. The false smiles. The deals being made behind champagne flutes.

"Thanks, Ray. I owe you one."

He hung up and went back inside to say his goodbyes.

Diesel Vaughn.

Now the real questions could begin.

FIVE

"OUR VICTIM IS DEAN "DIESEL" Vaughn," Savage told the team the next morning. "Ray let me know last night. He was a fully-patched member of the Crimson Angels."

"Except Rosalie and the other members claimed not to know him," Lucas reminded them.

"They're not going to help us." Sinclair turned to Savage. "Not unless you work your magic on Rosalie."

He snorted. "I tried. Now we'll have to see if she comes back with anything. There's a lot we can be getting on with, though." He nodded to the whiteboard. "First up, run Diesel's name through the database. My guess is he'll have a criminal record."

"Already on it," Thorpe said.

"Also, let's try to trace his next of kin. Any family he has around here, his friends, and so on. Maybe they can give us some insights. I want to piece together his last movements before he disappeared."

"It was over three years ago," Sinclair reminded him.

"I know, but someone will remember."

"What about Axle Weston?" Thorpe said. "You think he'll talk to us?"

"Doubt it. Not sure it's worth the drive out to the penitentiary. I thought I'd speak with Zeb first. He's been a club member for years, right back to when Axle was in charge."

"Recreational, though," Sinclair pointed out.

Savage scoffed. "In an outlaw MC, there's no such thing. Zeb's involved with that club up to his crooked eyeballs."

Looking at him now, Savage couldn't believe the man had once been a Denver cop. Even more crazy was that he'd actually saved Savage's life. Twice.

He owed him. That was probably the only reason why he hadn't arrested him yet. He kept threatening to, but Zeb always managed to stay just this side of the law.

"You were right, Diesel does have a record," Thorpe called out, as Savage headed for his office. He stopped, turned and walked back across the squadroom to his deputy's desk.

"Yeah? What for?"

"Assault, possession of an illegal firearm, and suspected arson, but he was never charged with that last one."

Savage frowned. "Who'd he beat up?"

Thorpe scanned the page. "He was in a bar fight, six years ago. Some guy called Nathan Woods."

"Could be something," Savage said. "Let's look this Nathan Woods character up. See if he's still around."

"This is interesting." Sinclair tapped her screen, before he'd had a chance to move on. "Diesel was bailed out by a woman named Honey Granger. Could be a girlfriend."

"Got an address?" he asked.

Sinclair's eyebrows shot up. "You're never going to believe this. Her last known address was the Hidden Gem Trailer Park."

Savage gave a snort. "Now isn't that a coincidence?"

Everyone knew how he felt about those.

· · ·

SAVAGE DROVE out of town and along the cracked two-lane road that led to the Hidden Gem trailer park. The sun was already high in the sky, scorching the tips of the pines, and he had the AC in the Suburban on full blast.

The trailer park sprawled out like a broken puzzle among the trees. He drove past the rows of dented mobile homes and doublewides, their yards cluttered with busted lawn chairs, kiddie pools half-filled with algae, and piles of scrap no one seemed in a hurry to move.

A man in a grease-streaked tank-top sat in a plastic chair outside one unit, whittling a block of wood. His eyes tracked the Suburban with the Sheriff's decal on the side. They narrowed in suspicion. Savage nodded to him and kept going.

He pulled up outside Zebediah Swift's mobile home, next to the Harley parked out front like a gleaming guard dog. After cutting the engine, he climbed out.

Damn, it was like a furnace out here.

Definitely one of the hottest summers since he'd been Sheriff. He wiped his brow and knocked on the door before stepping back.

Zeb answered a few seconds later, shirtless, wearing old jeans and a leather vest.

"Dalton." He squinted into the sun. "To what do I owe the pleasure?"

"How's it going, Zeb? Mind if we have a word?"

Zeb stepped aside and motioned him in. The inside of the mobile home was cooler on account of the air conditioner. The décor was masculine, and the place looked lived-in. A football game played quietly on the flat-screen in the corner.

"Drink?" Zeb offered.

"I'm working."

A shrug. "Suit yourself."

Savage followed him through to the kitchen, then leaned against the counter while Zeb took a beer out of the refrigerator. He popped the cap, then took a refreshing swig.

Savage got straight to it. "You ever know a guy named Dean Vaughn? His patch name was Diesel. I heard he was a... client." Amongst his other sides, Zeb ran an informal brothel out of a couple of trailers in his back yard.

Zeb paused, setting his beer down. "Diesel? Yeah, I knew him. Decent guy. Hell of a mechanic. Used to patch up all the club bikes back in the day."

"When's the last time you saw him?"

Zeb's forehead creased. "About three years ago. One day he just up and left. Rode out and never came back." He frowned. "Why? What happened to him?'

"How'd you know something happened?"

"Come on, man. How long have we been doing this?"

Savage sighed. Once a cop, always a cop. "He was shot. A couple of kids found his body in a dried-up lakebed outside of town."

Zeb whistled. "Shit."

There was a pause, then Zeb added, "Makes sense, though."

Savage frowned. "How come?"

"He was sweet on one of my girls. They were going to make a go of it, but he ran out on her too. I always thought it was strange at the time."

"Ran out on her?"

"Yeah, just took off. She was pretty cut up about it as I recall."

Savage frowned. "What happened to her?"

"No idea. She left right after he did. Said she didn't want to work here anymore. Who was I to stop her? She was a good kid, deserved a normal life. You know?"

Savage nodded. Fair enough. Zeb only employed girls who wanted the work. He'd never force anyone to stay if they wanted out.

"What was her name?"

Zeb took a long sip of his beer. "Honey. Honey Granger."

The woman who'd bailed Diesel out of jail.

Savage pursed his lips. "What can you tell me about her?"

A shrug. "Not much. Good kid, smarter than she made out. Don't know why she was working here, really. She could've done anything else. Still, times were tough and she was desperate."

Desperation drove people to do crazy things. That was one thing he'd learned in this business.

"I was glad when she got out."

Savage gave a slow nod. "Okay."

"Sure you don't want that beer? It's a scorcher today."

"Nah, I'm good. Thanks, man."

Savage bade him goodbye and stepped outside into the heat. Maybe it was his imagination, but it felt even hotter than before. He was nearly at the Suburban when his phone buzzed.

He glanced down at the screen. It was Sinclair.

"Hey, what's up?"

His deputy's voice was breathy and tense with suppressed excitement. "You're never going to guess what just happened."

"What?" Savage stopped, the sun beating down on his head. Not even the lazy old oak outside Zeb's offered any shade. Sun was at the wrong angle.

"Axle Weston just escaped from Fremont."

"What the hell?" he spluttered, staring out at the line of desolate trailers. "How?"

"Prison transfer. He was being moved to Colorado State Penitentiary, something to do with a beef he had with a member of a rival gang in lockup. They were ambushed and Axle escaped."

"Ambushed by who?" Savage said, but he already knew. A bad feeling circulated in his gut.

"Three big, tattooed guys in a van. They pulled on the driver and shot the guard. He'll live, but most of the prisoners got away."

"Shit. Sounds like the Crimson Angels."

"No doubt."

This was all they needed. Axle Weston heading this way to stir up trouble.

"You think he's going to come back here?" Sinclair asked.

"Yeah, where else would he go?"

Besides, Axle had a score to settle with Rosalie.

With him.

"You'd better watch your back," she told him, a worried edge to her voice. "Weston could be out for blood, since it was you who put him away."

"I'm not the one I'm worried about," he muttered.

SIX

ROSALIE WAS HAVING a bad fucking week. First the shit with the sheriff, and now her douchebag ex-husband had busted out of lockup. And as if that wasn't bad enough, from the sounds of things, he'd had help.

"Was it our guys?" she asked Scooter, her Sergeant at Arms, as she stalked back and forth across the bar. Hot rage rolled over her in waves, and she battled to keep it under control. It was early, the Roadhouse wasn't open yet, but this was where her office was, and she spent most mornings here, working, plotting, strategizing.

Scooter, jaw clenched, gave a half nod. "Looks like it. Word is Walt was in on it, probably arranged the whole thing."

"Fuck." Rosalie slammed a palm against the bar. "Of course it was that brown-noser."

Walt had never accepted her as President. The old-timer had been Axle's lapdog back in the day and was still clinging to the dumbass belief that a woman had no business running a 1% club. It didn't matter that under her rule, the club was leaner, meaner, and pulling in better money than Axle ever had.

The only thing her ex had brought to the club was chaos. When he'd been in charge, there'd been bar fights, pointless feuds, shit-loads of heat from law enforcement. Hell, one of their guys had even been murdered, his body dumped behind the bar in the parking lot. Talk about shitting in your own backyard.

Now there was Diesel.

By contrast, she brought order, discipline, profits. The club was prospering, its members thriving. They were a family again. Well, they had been before that idiot had gone and screwed it up.

"This is gonna be a fucking problem," she muttered.

"Soon this place will be crawling with U.S. Marshals," Scooter predicted, his mouth set in a grim line. Whilst initially skeptical, Axle's Sergeant at Arms and closest ally had switched sides and been loyal to her since she'd taken over. He'd had her back more times than she could count, but even he looked shaken.

This would affect him too. Axle hadn't taken Scooter's betrayal well. Rosalie had promoted him to VP and her judgment call had been correct. He was smart, tough, and didn't use violence unless it was absolutely necessary.

Brains before brawn, as she was fond of saying.

Rosalie paced the length of the bar, her heeled boots pounding the floor like war drums. "How could they be so fucking stupid? They may as well have spray-painted a big-ass bullseye on our backs. Jesus Christ."

She threw a glance over at Joel behind the bar. "Make sure there's no stash lying around. No dope, nothing in the backroom, nothing in the goddamn shitter. I want this place cleaner than a preacher's bed."

Joel nodded and got moving.

She turned back to Scooter. "I need to have a little talk with Walter. Where is that slack-jawed, backstabbing idiot?"

"Not back yet." Scooter crossed his arms. "Skully and Rourke rode out with him. I'm guessing all three were in on the ambush."

Rosalie's lip curled. "Fucking brilliant. Traitorous little pricks. You know what this means, right?"

Scooter gave a slow nod. "We've got a civil war on our hands."

"Damn right we do. They declared it the moment they backed Axle over me."

There was a line. Once crossed, there was no going back.

She planted both hands on the bar and leaned forward, glaring down the length of it like it was a firing line. She was so tense, her jaw ached from clenching it.

"If they want to back Axle, they can go rot in a jail cell with him. I've bled too much for this club to let some crusty has-beens drag us back into the dark ages. We keep tight, we ride strong, and if anyone asks, we don't know jack shit."

Scooter gave a grunt of agreement. "You want me to put some feelers out? See who's still with us?"

She nodded. "Yeah. I want to know where everyone stands. If they're with Axle, they're out. If they're with me, they better start acting like it."

Scooter didn't reply. The look in her eye said it all. Rosalie was ready for a war.

Turning, she stomped back to her office, pulling out her phone. Axle was going back inside, and she didn't care what she had to do to make that happen.

Taking a deep breath and hissing out a curse, she found Dalton Savage's number.

———

"DID YOU HEAR?" Savage heard the tension in Rosalie's voice.

"Yeah, just now. It's been all over the police radio."

"What the fuck?" she fumed.

"Was it your guys?" he asked.

She hesitated, and he knew it was true.

"They're no longer my guys," she said, after a beat. "I can't have him coming here and stirring up shit again, Dalton. I want him put away, back where he belongs."

"Unfortunately, the Marshals have jurisdiction. There's not much I can do on that front."

She hesitated. "I can give you their names."

Savage thought for a moment. "You got proof?"

"Not yet."

"Well, when you do, maybe we can talk. I can pass it on to the Marshals and they can take them in."

"They can't know it's from me," she said quickly.

"Obviously. That's what's going to make it tricky."

She sighed. "I'll think of something."

"Watch your back, Rosalie," he warned. "Axle's going to be gunning for you."

Her voice was grim. "I know."

They hung up. Not long after, Barb buzzed him.

"Sheriff, there are two officers from the U.S. Marshals Service here to see you."

Right on time.

"Send them in."

He stood as the door to his office opened and Barb showed the two Marshals in. They were both suited, broad-shouldered, with serious expressions that meant business. They shook hands, and the one with the mustache introduced himself as Chris Randall, his colleague as Bret Wiley.

"What can I do for you gentlemen?" Savage motioned for them to take a seat.

They did, then Randall spoke. "We've come to inform you that there's an escaped prisoner on the loose, and we think he's headed this way."

There was no point in pretending. "You're talking about Axle Weston?"

A bushy eyebrow arched in response. "So you've heard?"

"Hard not to. What makes you think he's coming to Hawk's Landing?"

"It's where he's from," Wiley said. "He has roots here. People who can help him disappear."

Savage regarded them both. "You think that's what he wants to do? Disappear?"

Randall frowned, his mustache turning down at the sides. "Don't you?"

Savage shrugged. "I think he wants to get revenge on his ex-wife, and possibly me. We're the ones who put him away in the first place."

There was a brief pause while that filtered in.

"We can assign someone—" Randall began, but Savage was already shaking his head.

"That won't be necessary, Marshal. I can look after myself, but if you want to bring him in, I'd suggest putting a tail on Rosalie Weston. He's likely to go there first, before he gets to me."

Randall nodded. "Thanks for the tip."

Rosalie wasn't going to like it, but she must be expecting it. It was no secret Axle had been the former president of the Crimson Angels, and he'd want to use his network to help him.

"Where can we find Mrs. Weston?" Wiley asked.

"Out at Mac's Roadhouse. That's a biker bar on the Durango Road. One piece of advice: Don't go there without backup."

Wiley glanced at his colleague.

Randall's jaw tightened. "That kind of biker bar?"

Savage gave a tight nod. "And then some."

AFTER THE MARSHALS LEFT, Thorpe came into his office.

"Boss, I've traced a next of kin for Honey Granger. Her mother lives in Durango. You want me to pay her a visit?"

Savage got to his feet. "No, that's okay. I want to pay Shelby a visit. Give him a head's up. I'll stop by her place on the way."

Thorpe nodded. "I'll send you the address."

Sheriff Shelby had become a good friend over the years. He and

Becca had been over to his place for supper a couple of times. He drew in a breath as the familiar pang of regret kicked him in the gut.

Damned if he didn't miss Becca—and Connor.

If the Marshals caught Axle sooner rather than later, he might be able to get to Pagosa Springs and visit them this weekend. The thought made him feel better.

Phyllis Granger lived in a small house on the outskirts of Durango. Close enough to walk into the town center, but far enough away not to be too pricey. It had a neat front porch, a tidy yet barren yard, and a functional, but unpainted wooden fence around the property. It was clear the family didn't have much money but made the best of what they did have.

When Mrs. Granger opened the door, he knew his first impressions had been right. Slim, dark hair tied back, and wearing shorts with a faded but clean T-shirt, she looked both efficient and practical.

"Mrs. Granger?" he enquired.

"Yes?" Her gaze fell to his badge. "You're not our Sheriff."

"No, ma'am. My name's Dalton Savage, and I'm the Sheriff of Hawk's Landing. Do you have a moment to talk?"

"Sure. Come in."

She gestured for him to follow her into the house. He stepped into a sparsely decorated living room, clean and tidy, with a vase of colorful flowers on the table visible in the adjoining dining room. "Now, what brings the sheriff of Hawk's Landing to my door?"

"It's concerning your daughter, Mrs. Granger."

She stiffened, her eyes widening in alarm. "My daughter? Why? Has something happened to Honey?"

"No, ma'am. We'd like to ask her some questions about her late boyfriend, Dean Vaughn."

"Late boyfriend? You mean Dean's dead?" Her gaze hardened.

"Yes. His body was recently found in a dried-out lakebed." She didn't need to know the gory details.

"Oh, my—" Her hand fluttered to her chest. "We all thought he'd run off without her."

"Without her?" His understanding was that they'd wanted to settle down together. Here, in Hawk's Landing. "You mean they were planning on running away together?"

"Yeah. She didn't tell me at the time, only after he disappeared. Said they were planning to elope. They wanted to be together, but what with him in that terrible motorcycle club—" She glanced down, leaving the sentence unfinished.

No explanation needed. Savage got the picture.

"But he never did?"

"No, sir. My Honey waited, bags packed and everything, but he never showed. I wasn't here at the time, but she told me afterwards. Said he never came for her, so we just figured he'd left without her."

"Was that like him?"

"To leave her? No. Say what you will about that boy, but he was sweet on my Honey. Plain for all to see."

Savage gave a thoughtful nod. "You didn't wonder if something happened to him?"

She shrugged. "Well, yeah, but he didn't go back to the club. When Honey asked them if they'd seen him, she got the same story. He'd just up and vanished. Nobody knew where he was."

"I see. Did Honey try to find him?"

"No. He broke her heart, poor thing. It was a tough time." She sighed, lowering her head. "We never for a moment imagined he was dead."

Savage frowned. "I need to talk to her, Mrs. Granger."

"My Honey is doing good now," her mother said. "This will just bring it all up again."

"Don't you think she deserves to know what really happened to him?"

"I suppose." A moment passed. "How'd he die?"

"He was shot."

She bit her lip. "I don't want my daughter mixed up in anything to do with those outlaws. They're bad news."

He nodded, but said, "I'm sorry, but I still need to talk to her. Where's she living, Mrs. Granger?"

Reluctantly, "She's living here. With me."

Just then, he heard footsteps and turned to see a toddler, about three years old, walk into the room. He had soft, brown hair and enormous, long-lashed eyes.

"Nana, I'm hungry."

Mrs. Granger smiled. "My grandson, Sheriff. Ben, say hello to Sheriff Savage."

"Hello." The boy gave a toothy smile. "Are you hungry too?"

Savage nodded. "Actually, yeah. I am, but I'm working, so I can't eat just yet."

"Poor you," the boy said, turning back to his grandma.

"I've got your lunch ready," she told him, scooping him up. He wriggled, but she carried him over to the table and set him on a chair. "Stay there. I'll be right back."

"When will your daughter be home?" Savage called after her, as she disappeared into the kitchen.

A moment later, she reappeared, carrying a small plate of food. "Her shift finishes at five. She works at Lou's Diner up on Main."

He knew Lou's.

"Thank you, Mrs. Granger. You've been very helpful. Don't worry, I can show myself out."

"Don't know what good it's going to do you," she called, as he turned to leave. "Neither me nor Honey have seen Dean in over three years, and we sure as hell haven't spoken to any of his biker friends."

"Just doing my job, ma'am. Thanks again." Savage left her to her grandson and walked out of the house and back to his Suburban.

Before he pulled away, he got on the police radio. "Sinclair, take Lucas and get over to Lou's Diner on Main in Durango. Apparently, Honey Granger is on shift until five o'clock. I'm going to pay Shelby a visit."

"On our way."

SEVEN

SINCLAIR, with Lucas driving the cruiser, pulled up outside Lou's Diner. "I've never seen the place so dry," Lucas had commented on the way over. The scrub grass along the roadside had browned to a brittle yellow, and the red rock hills in the distance looked scorched under the sun. "It's like a tinderbox waiting to go up."

"Don't say that," she'd snapped, thinking about Mason out in the field with his crew. The wildfires were spreading, and Mason and his teams were working around the clock to keep them contained. She hadn't seen her Fire Chief boyfriend in days, and he'd sounded exhausted on the phone last night.

Except now she felt bad. The rookie deputy had only been trying to make conversation.

"I'm sorry I jumped down your throat back there," she said, hoping to clear the air. "I'm just worried about Mason. He hasn't had a break since this first started."

"I get it, don't worry. Sorry I brought it up."

She nodded.

"You do a lot of business in Durango?" Lucas asked as he got out of the cruiser.

"When we need to, but it's Sheriff Shelby's jurisdiction. Sometimes our business overlaps, then we join forces."

"Like the protest outside the Boulder Creek Hotel last year?"

"Exactly."

That was the first time she'd met Lucas McBride. His aunt, Clara, had led the protest that had turned violent. A Philadelphia thug, Romano Caruso, had holed up inside, having taken Sinclair hostage. It was Savage's partner, Becca, who'd talked him down, only for him to be gunned down on the sidewalk outside the hotel.

She shook her head at the memory. "That was one crazy day."

"It sure was." They walked toward the diner. "Let's go see what Honey has to say."

Inside was bright and bustling, with sleek chrome fixtures, light wood tables, and a long counter lined with cushioned stools. Sunlight streamed in the street-facing windows, and they could smell coffee and grilled food.

"Smells good," Lucas said, looking around.

A rotund man with a receding hairline stood by the front desk, seating people who came in.

"Hi there. Could you tell me where to find Honey Granger?" Sinclair asked, holding up her badge.

He glanced at it, then nodded over his shoulder. "She's serving table five. Want me to get her for you?"

"Please. We'll wait here."

He nodded and wove through the tight arrangement of tables, through the bustle of customers and servers, to a blond woman wearing jeans, a T-shirt, and a red apron with Lou's written in cursive on the front. He pointed over at them, and they saw Honey's smile fade. Frowning, she made her way over.

"Deputies, what's this about? Has something happened to my mother? To Ben?" They could read the anxiety on her face.

"Everyone's fine," Sinclair assured her, watching her shoulders sag in relief. "We're here with some news about your former boyfriend, Dean Vaughn."

DUST DEVIL

"Dean?" she blinked, and Sinclair noticed she had big, very pretty, brown eyes. "I haven't thought about him in years. What news?"

Sinclair cleared her throat. "I'm sorry to tell you this, but his body was recently discovered in a dried-up lake outside Hawk's Landing."

She gasped, her hand flying to her mouth. "Oh, my God! Dean's dead?"

Sinclair nodded.

"But... I don't understand. How?"

"He was shot."

Honey stared at them, but she'd started shaking.

"Let' s sit down." Sinclair gestured to an empty table.

Honey eased her petite frame into a chair, but her cheeks had lost their natural flush.

"Would you like a glass of water?" Lucas asked.

She nodded, fine white teeth quivering over her lower lip.

He went to fetch one, while Sinclair sat opposite her, a haunted look on Honey's face.

"When... when did he die?"

"At least three years ago."

"Oh, God." Honey shook her head. "I can't believe this. I thought... I thought he'd run out on me. I should have known Dean wouldn't do that." Tears welled in her eyes.

Sinclair studied the clearly distraught young woman. "You thought he'd left town?" Savage had outlined what Honey's mother had said on the phone, but she wanted to confirm the stories.

"Yeah. We wanted to get married, but when he didn't pick me up, I thought he'd changed his mind. Run out on his responsibility."

"You were pregnant?" Sinclair asked, again knowing the answer.

Another nod. One tear escaped and ran down her face. She reached for a napkin.

Sinclair imagined the pregnant young woman waiting for her

43

boyfriend to arrive and how crushed she must have been when he didn't.

"You didn't think it was strange when he didn't show up? That something might have happened to him?" It was the same question Savage had asked, but they had to know why she'd just accepted that he'd run off.

"I did, at first, but then I asked the guys at the club. His buddies hadn't seen him either. Nobody knew where he was. Everybody assumed he'd taken off, skipped town."

Lucas came back with the water. She nodded her thanks and took a shaky sip. "I can't believe he's been dead all this time. Poor Dean."

"I'm sorry for your loss," Sinclair said. "But do you mind if I ask you some more questions? It's important for us to understand what happened."

Honey sniffed and nodded. Lucas stood by the table, letting them talk. Sinclair appreciated his discretion. He was insightful, and smart. He was going to make a fine deputy.

"Where did you two meet?" Sinclair asked. Of course, she knew about Zeb, but she wanted to see if Honey would lie about her previous occupation.

"Do you mind if I don't say right now?" She glanced over her shoulder to see whether her boss was watching.

"It's okay. I know about Zeb's," Sinclair said.

Honey swallowed. "It was a while back and I was in a bad place. I've cleaned up since then." Her voice was a low whisper, and Sinclair could tell she was nervous.

"I can see that," she encouraged.

"Everything changed when I found out I was pregnant." Honey stared at her hands. "I didn't tell Dean at first, but when he asked why I wasn't working there anymore, I had to tell him."

"Were—Were you sure it was his?" Sinclair asked. Given her occupation at the time, it was something they had to clarify.

Honey nodded. "He was the only one where—" She faded out, looking around helplessly.

"That's okay." She got the picture. "Is that when he suggested you two elope?"

"Yes," she whispered, giving a sad nod. "We had to run away because the club wouldn't let him go."

"How'd you know that?" Sinclair asked sharply.

"Dean told me. He wanted out, but Axle, the club president, said no. He told him there was no out." She shook her head. "We had no choice."

Sinclair shared a look with Lucas before turning back to Honey. "Was Dean acting strangely at all before you guys were due to leave town?"

Her eyes hardened. "Yeah, he was pissed with Axle. He just wanted to be with me and to get on with his life—and that bastard wouldn't let him. The club was like a noose around his throat. I hated them."

"Do you know if Dean was involved in anything illegal?" Sinclair asked.

Honey hesitated, then sighed. "They were always dragging him into some shady activity. It was dangerous stuff. He could have been arrested, or worse." She gulped. "I guess the worse did happen. I just didn't know."

"Do you know what he was involved in before he disappeared?" Sinclair asked, leaning forward. "What shady activities?"

"Not exactly." Honey gripped the water. "Dean didn't talk to me about club business."

"You're sure? You can't remember anything?"

Her forehead crinkled. "I remember Dean saying they'd had an argument, but he never told me what it was about."

"You mean him and Axle?"

Honey nodded.

Sinclair gnawed on her lip. From what they'd discovered, Dean had been a member of the outlaw MC for nearly a decade at that point. It must have been hard to leave. He must have really loved Honey to put her before the club.

"Do you think Axle could have killed Dean because he was set on leaving the club?" Sinclair asked, wanting to gauge Honey's reaction.

This time a plump, sad tear did roll down her cheek. "I hope not," she whispered, "but it's possible. Right?"

Yeah, it was.

Honey looked up as a group of teens walked in. They hovered at the entrance, looking for a place to sit. "Can I get back to work now?'

Sinclair nodded. "Sure. Thanks, Honey. You've been very helpful."

The young woman got up, then hesitated. "What will happen to Dean's body?"

Sinclair also got to her feet. "After the ME has finished the autopsy, it'll be released to his next of kin. Probably his parents."

"His mother lives in Houston," Honey murmured. "Dean never knew who his father was." She blinked away the tears. "That's why he wanted to marry me. He wanted to do a better job than his dad had done with him."

Sinclair put a gentle hand on her shoulder. "I'm sorry," she murmured, again.

Honey sniffed. "Thank you."

They let her get back to work and headed for the door. Lucas held it open.

"What do you think?" Sinclair asked, once they'd stepped outside.

He pursed his lips. "She's obviously upset. I think she was telling the truth about not knowing he was dead."

"Yeah, me too." Sinclair frowned as they walked to the cruiser. "Those tears were real."

Lucas nodded. "I think it's time to take a closer look at Axle Weston."

EIGHT

ROSALIE HEARD the rumble before she saw the bikers turn off the Durango Road and into the Roadhouse lot. Deep and low, it sent a ripple of anger through her body, and she clenched her fists.

They were back.

Scooter heard it too and clicked his fingers. They'd been waiting for this moment. Hank, the barrel-chested ex-con who'd taken over from Scooter as Sergeant at Arms, along with six other loyal club members, made their way outside, weapons drawn.

Before Rosalie stepped out, she muttered something to Joel, whose eyes widened, but he gave a quick nod and disappeared back inside.

They stood in an arrow formation, Rosalie in front, as four motorcycles roared into the gravel lot.

Axle Weston dismounted, peeling off a matte-black full-face helmet. His beard was scruffier, grayer than she remembered, but the cocky grin beneath it was exactly the same.

"Hello, Rosie," he said, his mouth twisting into a sneer.

Behind him stood Walter, heavyset and sweating, his eyes sweeping the line of men. Rourke, tall and twitchy as ever, came to a halt beside them, leather jacket creaking with every step. Skully hung back, a human pit bull with a shaved head and a too-eager look in his eye.

"You're not welcome here," she said in a tight voice.

Axle spread his arms. "Come on, babe. Is that any way to greet your old man?"

Rosalie couldn't believe he had the audacity to come here, but then, Axle had never lacked balls. That was never his problem.

"I don't think you heard me, Axle. You and your co-conspirators are not welcome here."

Walter's expression hardened. "What do you mean, co-conspirators?"

She kept her voice calm, steady, despite the thumping of her heart. "I'm sorry, Walt. Did you just think you could betray me and then come back with Axle like nothing had happened?"

His face twisted into a perturbed scowl. "We busted him out. That's all."

"You sprung him so he could come back and kill me." She glanced at Axle. "Ain't that right... babe?"

She could tell by the mean glint in his eyes that she'd hit the nail on the head.

Walt's face dropped. "Hold up—what? No one said nothin' about killin' anybody."

Walter was a fool.

"You set me up, didn't you?" Axle scoffed, glaring at Rosalie. "I always suspected it was you. You sold me out to the Sheriff. Couldn't wait to sit in Daddy's chair?"

Rosalie heard a low murmur and knew she had to put a stop to that rumor ASAP. "It was your own stupidity that got you locked up, Axle. What? Did you think you could just drive the Sheriff's pregnant fiancée off the road and there wouldn't be consequences?" She gave a brittle laugh. "He was gunning for you. I had nothing to do with it."

The murmurs quieted down. They all knew Axle had nearly killed the Sheriff's fiancée two years ago. Not many of them knew she'd been pregnant at the time. As badass as some of them were, you didn't mess with pregnant women.

"In fact, I cleaned up your mess. The Sheriff has pretty much left us alone since you went down. We've been doing good without you. Better than ever."

"That's right," Scooter echoed.

There were murmurs of approval now.

"Ah, yes. How quickly you switched sides, Scooter. Couldn't wait to climb up the ladder, eh? Did you take my place in her bed, too?"

Beside her, she felt Scooter bristle. "Easy," she whispered.

"I'm surprised you've got the audacity to come back here," Rosalie said. "Being a wanted felon and all."

He smirked. "I'm not hanging around. Just wanted to drop by and say hey, that's all."

"Well, you've done that. Now you can leave."

"You going to make me, Rosie?"

At that point, Joel came out of the clubhouse and caught her eye. He gave an infinitesimal nod.

Axle smirked. "I'd like to see you try."

Rosalie didn't flinch. She wanted to pull the Glock from her hip and end this, but she was smarter than that. Cooler. More dangerous when she didn't explode. The rest of the men who flanked her had their weapons poised, ready to fire.

"You've got sixty seconds to get off my property," she said, eyes locked on his.

Axle chuckled, like she'd told him a dirty joke. "You always had balls, Rosie. Shame you've forgotten who you're talking to."

Scooter stepped forward. "She didn't forget. We just stopped giving a shit."

Axle's eyes flicked to Scooter, then to the others now flanking Rosalie like a wall. For the first time, that cocksure glint dimmed. Just a fraction.

"I'll be back for you, Rosie. You can count on it." He climbed back on his Harley-Davidson. Walter, Rourke, and Skully didn't follow right away.

"Last chance, gentlemen," Rosalie called after them. "You want to stay in the club, you come inside now. Go with him and don't bother coming back. Ever."

All three hesitated. Axle gave them a scathing look like they'd stabbed him in the back. When none of them made a move to follow him, he gave a slow nod, then revved his engine and moved forward.

Rosalie snorted. She'd known they wouldn't go. The club was their family. It gave them a sense of belonging, a purpose. They'd be lost without it.

"You'll pay for this, Rosalie," Axle threatened, stopping right in front of her.

Then—

Sirens could be heard on the Durango Road, approaching fast.

"You called the cops on me?" he asked incredulously.

"I warned you not to mess with me." She tossed her hair over her shoulder and flipped him off.

Axle didn't retaliate. There wasn't time. With a loud roar, he sped out of the lot, toward Durango. Seconds later, two police cars from the U.S. Marsha Service turned in, while one raced off after the lone biker.

"Get inside," she told Walt, Rourke, and Skully. "I'll handle this."

Everybody else went into the bar except for Scooter, who stuck to her side.

Despite what she'd said to the Sheriff, she wouldn't give up her men, not now they were back in the fold. She'd won back their loyalty, and now they owed her. That was far more valuable than having them out there teaming up with Axle and plotting revenge.

Steeling herself, she turned to face the Marshals.

NINE

"SHE CLAIMED none of her men were responsible," U.S. Marshal Randall told Savage the next morning. They stood in Savage's office, the sun streaming in through the open blinds. It was going to be another scorcher of a day.

He frowned. Strange. Rosalie had insisted she knew who'd helped Axle Weston break out, so why would she hold back now? Unless she couldn't prove it, or she wanted to protect the club members for some reason. Knowing Rosalie, she was working an angle.

"Maybe they weren't," he said, even though his words lacked conviction.

The marshal shrugged. "You were right, though. Weston made a bee-line for Mac's Roadhouse. Took off just as we got there."

"You lost him?" Savage asked, jaw tightening.

"Yeah. He took off on his damn Harley and we lost him in the backstreets of Durango. Got the motorcycle, though, so he's on foot now. He won't get far without help."

"You got the Crimson Angels under surveillance?" Savage asked. "If anyone's going to help him, it's one of them."

"Got a tail on his ex-wife, like you suggested, and some of the key players. A guy called Scooter, the Vice President, and Hank Stevens, who appears to be their enforcer. Stevens has a record, so we're particularly interested in him."

"He's also loyal to Rosalie," Savage told him. "You're better off looking at some of the older guys like Skully and Walt Minstrel. They've got records too and were close to Axle."

"Skully?" Randall typed the names into his phone.

"Can't remember his first name, but it'll be on file."

Randall nodded. "Unfortunately, we can't keep tabs on all of them. Resources are limited and there are over a dozen club members."

"Understood. If I hear anything, I'll let you know. Did you ever find out where that tip-off came from yesterday?"

"Nah, but we pinged the call. It came from the vicinity of the Roadhouse. Couldn't get an exact match, since it was off by then."

Typical. Savage was willing to bet it had been Rosalie. She was desperate to see Axle back behind bars, where he belonged.

AFTER THE U.S. MARSHAL had left, Savage called a briefing to discuss the case. The AC was back on, thank God, and he stood in front of the vent, relishing the coolness between his shoulder blades.

"What do we know about Dean Vaughn?" He turned to Sinclair who was fanning herself with a piece of paper. "You get anything from Honey Granger?"

"Yeah, she seemed genuinely shocked by the news," Sinclair said, putting the paper down on her desk. Lucas backed her up with a nod. "We don't think she knew he'd been murdered."

"She did say he'd had an altercation with Axle, though," Lucas piped up. "But she didn't know what it was about."

"Could have been about him leaving the club," Savage mused.

"That was obviously a factor, but she wasn't sure."

"Anything else?" Savage asked.

Sinclair shook her head. "She was very upset by the news."

"Understandable. He was the father of her child. She'd hoped to marry him." Savage turned to Thorpe. "Anything on that guy Diesel got into the bar fight with?"

"Yeah. He was a logger named Nathan Woods. At the time of the assault, he worked for John Littleton's company."

Savage arched an eyebrow. "Is he still around?"

"Actually, yeah. According to the DMV records, he lives out on Forest Drive. Littleton is still listed as his employer."

"That's something we can follow up, at least." Savage glanced over at Sinclair. "What about Dean Vaughn's next of kin?"

"We found out his mother lives in Houston," she provided. "Father's deceased."

"That matches with what I found," Thorpe agreed.

"Okay." Savage rubbed his jaw, thinking. "Lucas, can you get the mother on the line and ask her if Dean contacted her at all before he disappeared? Find out if she knew about his relationship with Honey Granger."

"Will do," the Deputy nodded.

"You got an address for Nathan Woods?" Savage asked Thorpe, who held up a sticky note with the contact details written on it.

Savage gave a pleased grin, snapped it out of his hand, and turned to Sinclair. "Let's go pay Nathan Woods a visit."

THE FOREST ROAD wound through the foothills. Normally green and full of life, they were now a dull gold and faded brown. The grasses along the edges were dry and brittle, and the pine trees looked dusty, their needles dulled by weeks without rain.

The wildfires were a constant worry. Even out here, it wouldn't take much to set it off.

They rounded a bend, and the trees gave way to a clearing where

L.T. RYAN

a squat, weather-worn cabin sat back from the road. The place was plain and practical. Wood siding faded to gray, a tin roof patched in spots, and a stump out front that looked like it doubled as a chopping block. A beat-up pickup sat under a lean-to, its bed full of coiled rope, gas cans, and a few lengths of fresh-cut pine.

"Looks like he's home." Sinclair pulled in behind the truck.

Savage got out and scanned the area. A half-full clothesline hung between two posts, jeans stiff from the sun. A woodpile sat neatly stacked near the porch, and a dog barked once from somewhere behind the house. "Let's see."

They walked up the steps onto the wooden porch, the dry boards creaking under their weight. Savage knocked twice on the screen door.

A few seconds passed, then a man filled the doorway. Broad shoulders, sun-reddened skin, plaid shirt with the sleeves rolled up. He looked like a lifelong logger. His beard was patchy, hair flattened like he'd just taken off a cap.

"Nathan Woods?" Savage asked.

The screen door creaked open. "Yeah."

"Sheriff's Office." Savage flashed his badge. "I'm Sheriff Savage. This is Deputy Sinclair. We've got a few questions, if you don't mind."

Nathan eyed them both, then shrugged and stepped aside. "Come on in."

Savage walked in followed by Sinclair. He glanced at the small table littered with mail and a half-eaten sandwich. Seemed they'd interrupted Nathan Woods during his lunch break.

"Won't take long," Savage said, not sitting down. "We're looking into the death of a man named Dean Vaughn. You know him?"

Nathan's jaw tightened. "Yeah, I know him. Didn't know he'd passed, though."

"How'd you meet?" Savage asked.

"We got into a fight at Miller's Walk. He knocked me out, and the cops came. He got arrested."

54

"What was the fight about?" Sinclair asked. Miller's Walk was the name of a rowdy bar in Hawk's Landing and one of the few watering holes in the town.

"A chick. What else?"

Sinclair frowned. "Which woman?"

"Some whore—" At Sinclair's penetrating look, he cleared his throat. "I mean some girl he was seeing out at the Hidden Gem Trailer Park."

"He was jealous?" she asked.

"You could say that. Don't know why. She wasn't that special."

Sinclair's jaw tightened, but she was experienced enough not to react.

"You see him after that?" Savage cut in.

"No. I ain't seen him for years. Like I said, I didn't even know he'd died. What happened, anyway?" He looked between the two of them.

"He was shot," Savage said, matter-of-factly. "We're talking to anyone who might have had a beef with him."

Nathan held up his hands. "Whoa! Hang on a minute. I had nothing to do with that. Didn't even know the guy."

"You got into a fight with him," Savage reminded him.

"No way. He attacked me. I was just sitting at the bar minding my own business and he came in, stormed over, and punched my lights out."

That was what the police report had said.

"He say anything?" Savage prompted.

"Yeah. He yelled at me to stay away from her, then he hit me. Dude was out of control, man. Definite anger management issues. Not surprised he got himself shot."

Savage glanced at Sinclair, who shrugged. The logger's account matched what they already knew. "Okay, that's it for now. We'll let you get back to your lunch."

"There was another guy with him," Nathan added, as they were about to leave.

Savage turned. "Who?"

"Think his name was Scooter. I see him around town on occasion, although he mostly hangs out at the Roadhouse. He's one of those Crimson Angels too."

"Scooter was there?" Sinclair repeated.

"Yeah, that's what I said."

"What was he doing?" Savage asked.

"Standing by the door. Watching his buddy's back. You know those biker dudes, they stick together."

That was true. Members of the MC seldom went anywhere alone.

Savage nodded. "We'll be in touch if we need to ask you anything else."

Outside, Sinclair muttered, "Guy's a misogynistic asshole. I'm sorry, but he deserved to get punched."

Savage agreed but didn't say as much.

"Interesting about Scooter," he said, as they got into the cruiser. "Let's bring him in for questioning."

"Are you going back to the Roadhouse to get him?" Sinclair asked, turning onto the road back to Hawk's Landing. "Or am I?"

Savage smirked. "Might be better to pick him up at his place, if we have an address for him."

"I'm sure Thorpe can track it down."

As his deputy drove, Savage wondered if Rosalie had any information for him yet, or if she had even bothered to ask. After backtracking on her pledge to give the marshals the names of the men responsible for busting Axle out of prison, he wasn't convinced of her commitment.

It was on the way back to the Sheriff's Office that they got the call from Barb. Mason was on the line and asking to be put through to the Sheriff. Sinclair shot him a worried look.

"That's not good," she whispered.

"Put him through," Savage ordered.

Mason's voice came over the radio. They both heard the strain. "Sheriff, the wildfire is gaining traction. It won't be long before it gets out of hand. I think we should issue an evacuation warning for houses in the vicinity."

"Okay, I'll handle it," Savage said grimly. "What else do you need?"

"More fighters would be good, and it's time to call in the choppers to drop water on the burn zones. It's above what we can handle on the ground. My men also need fresh supplies. We've been working double shifts and they're exhausted."

"I'll see if I can organize some additional resources," he said, already thinking about Shelby and the Durango Fire Department, and that recent goodwill visit to Councilman Beckett's office. "Is this thing going to grow, or can we get it under control?"

"If we double our efforts and get the water bombs, we might be able to hold it back," Mason said, weariness threading through his voice. "But it could go either way."

Sinclair pressed harder on the gas, and the cruiser surged forward. "Stay safe out there," she called before the line cut out.

Savage clicked the mic. Change of plans. "Barb, ask Thorpe to bring in Scooter for questioning. Send Lucas out to the fire zone and patch me through to Sheriff Shelby."

"Sure thing," came Barb's efficient reply. Static crackled, then the line clicked.

"Shelby," said the Durango sheriff.

"Hey, it's Dalton." Savage gripped the door handle as Sinclair took a tight turn on a narrow backroad. "We've got a situation down here, and I need a hand. Brushfire's jumped containment lines. We're issuing a precautionary evacuation warning for the homes backing onto the state forest near Hawk's Landing. Our FD's stretched thin. Can you help us out?"

"Yeah, sure thing," he said without hesitation. "I've got personnel I can send, and I'll get in touch with the brush unit. They're standing by, so they'll be able to loan you some boots, too. The chopper's trickier. We'll need to run that through Colorado Fire Management. They handle air resources statewide."

"Understood. I'll make the call. Appreciate the backup."

He hung up just as Sinclair swung onto a smaller forest service road. The cruiser bumped over hard-packed dirt, passing a cluster of older homes tucked close to the timberline. Many had wooden siding and dry brush piled close to the structures. The place was a tinder box waiting to go up.

The sharp, bitter smell of smoke floated across on the breeze that was picking up now, swirling dust and dried pine needles along the roadside.

"Perfect conditions for a flare-up," Sinclair muttered, as she turned on the overhead lights, and the red-and-blues flickered through the hazy afternoon light.

They pulled up in front of the first house. A dog barked from behind a screen door, and a man in a sweat-stained T-shirt stepped out onto the porch, shielding his eyes.

"Afternoon." Savage stepped out of the cruiser and flashed his badge. "You're in a potential fire zone. We're issuing a precautionary evacuation warning. I suggest you start packing essentials—documents, medications," he glanced down, "pets."

The man's gaze drifted toward the ridge where a faint column of smoke curled skyward. "It that close already?"

"It's a precautionary measure," he explained. "The ground's dry and the wind is picking up. We don't want to take any chances."

They split up and moved door to door. Knock, flash the badge, deliver the warning. Most people were compliant, some already had packed bags by the door, aware the fire was creeping ever closer.

Savage was climbing back into the cruiser when the radio chirped with a loud burst of static, followed by a voice from dispatch.

"All units, be advised. A local wildfire alert has been issued in Hawk's Landing. Level One evacuations in place for zones east of State Route 160. Maintain situational awareness and proceed with caution."

"That's us," said Sinclair, getting in behind the wheel.

He nodded. Barb had contacted the local radio station and sent out the alert. "Let's pick up the pace."

She threw the cruiser into gear, tires kicking up dust as they continued down the winding lane. Smoke blurred the sky in streaks, and somewhere behind the treeline, the fire moved unseen—quiet for now but coming.

TEN

THE AIR STANK OF SMOKE.

Savage stood on the gravel street shoulder and squinted toward the hills. A wall of grey haze drifted from the treeline, the scent acrid and urgent. Ash floated like snowflakes on the wind.

The fire crews were fully engaged along the active fire edge, trying to hold the line. Engines were staged on the flanks, hoses deployed, while hand crews cut firebreaks along the ridge in case the winds shifted.

Savage had called in mutual aid from both the Durango and Pagosa departments, and the Colorado Fire Management Task Force had deployed. Above them, twin-engine tankers were circling low over the ridge, dropping chemical retardant like red rain.

Evacuations had expanded beyond the first defense zone. Residents from the second and third rows of homes were being escorted out, loaded into vans and trucks organized by local churches and community organizations. The evacuation order was now mandatory, and the road out of Hawk's Ridge crawled with headlights, panicked drivers, and families clutching what little they'd grabbed.

The whole scene pulsed with tension.

Savage checked his watch. They'd been on the line most of the afternoon, and the sun now sank low over the mountains, a smoky fireball just visible through the haze.

"I'm heading back," he said when it looked like the teams had made some headway. "Scooter's waiting, and we've only got so long to interview him."

Sinclair opted to stay behind to assist Mason and coordinate the evacuation logistics. Lucas stayed too, helping where he could, while smokejumpers deployed to a hot spot flaring near the ridgeline.

BACK AT THE Sheriff's office, an impatient Scooter sat in the interview room, arms folded, a bottle of water in front of him. He wasn't cuffed because this wasn't an arrest. He wasn't even under caution. The guy could have walked at any time, yet he'd waited. That said something.

"About time," he muttered, as Savage walked in and set a photograph face-down on the table. He'd grabbed a quick shower and changed his clothes, but he couldn't get rid of the sour taste in his mouth or the smell of smoke in his hair.

"Got diverted to the wildfire," Savage replied, figuring since the guy had stayed, he owed him that much. Besides, Scooter could probably smell the smoke on him.

The biker gave a grumpy shrug as if to say, "that's not my problem."

Savage studied him across the table. He looked like he'd stepped out of a motorcycle magazine. Black leather vest, tattoos coiled down his forearms, a permanent scowl etched into his hard, weathered face.

"Thanks for waiting."

Scooter snorted but didn't otherwise respond.

Savage turned the photograph over and slid it across the table. Diesel's old mugshot. Not an attractive image, but better than the crime scene photos. "Dean Vaughn. You knew him?"

Scooter stared at the image, blinked, then said, "Yeah. I knew Diesel."

"When's the last time you saw him?"

He only hesitated for a second. "About three years ago. Right before he disappeared."

"You were there when he got into a bar fight with Nathan Woods." It wasn't a question.

Scooter's lips curled. "That wasn't a fight. Diesel rearranged the guy's face for talking shit about Honey."

Savage nodded. "Nathan Woods pressed charges, and Diesel was arrested for assault."

A shrug. "Guy deserved it. He was a prick."

Same sentiment as Sinclair.

"Honey bailed him out. Did you know the two of them were gonna run off together? That Diesel wanted out?"

"Yeah. Sure, I knew. We all did. Said he was done with the club life. Wanted to settle down, start fresh. Maybe open a garage somewhere."

"I'm guessing Axle didn't take it well?"

Scooter's eyes darkened. "Hell no. According to Axle, no one walks away from the Angels unless they're in a box."

Interesting.

"Did he threaten him?"

Scooter leaned back in the chair. "They argued about it, sure. Axle wanted to make an example out of Diesel. I told him to let it go. Diesel wasn't snitching, just leaving to start over, but that didn't make any difference to Axle."

Savage narrowed his eyes. "You think Axle killed him?"

Scooter hesitated. "I don't know. The two of them used to be tight, you know? I can't see Axle putting a bullet through him. But a few days later, Diesel was gone. We all figured he'd bolted, but now?" He exhaled hard. "Shit."

Savage studied him, considering this. Like Scooter, he wasn't sure Axle would assassinate a buddy, especially one he went way

DUST DEVIL

back with. Not unless Diesel knew something Axle didn't want getting out. "Before he disappeared, did Diesel mention running any side errands, any jobs he was doing? Anyone he was looking into?"

Scooter's eyebrows twinged. "Yeah, actually. Now that you mention it. He asked me once about Larry Jeffries."

"Jeffries? The former sheriff?"

"Your predecessor, yeah. Said he was a corrupt fucker and that Axle had asked him to look into it."

It was hardly news.

Everybody knew the old sheriff had been dirty. Misappropriation of funds and allegations of embezzlement, but nothing had stuck. It had taken a federal warrant to bring him down, and Savage had been instrumental in making that happen.

"Think Diesel was going to blow the whistle on something?" Savage asked.

Scooter shook his head. "Nah, he wasn't the type. Didn't give a shit what others were doing. He just did what Axle asked him to, no questions asked."

"You think it could have been something Axle was involved in that got him killed?" Savage asked, more to himself than Scooter.

The biker shrugged and shifted in his chair. "That's your job, Sheriff. Now, if we're done here, I'd like to get the hell out."

Savage thanked him for his time and walked him out.

Larry Jefferies. That was a new angle. Something he fully intended to look into, as soon as they got the wildfires under control and the town was safe again.

SAVAGE HAD LEFT the office and was on his way back to the fire line to check on how the crews were doing when Barb got on the radio.

"Dalton, Rosalie just called. Someone took a shot at her."

His breath caught. "She okay?"

"Yeah, says it's a flesh wound, but she sounded pretty pissed off."

L.T. RYAN

He could imagine.

"I'm on the Durango Road. I'll swing by there on my way."

Two heavyset bikers armed with shotguns were pacing up and down outside the Roadhouse when he pulled up. They gave him hard looks, but Savage simply nodded at them and marched into the bar.

Rosalie sat at a table, a bandage wrapped around her upper arm. Her face was pinched with pain. Or maybe it was barely contained rage. Joel sat opposite her, packing away a first aid kid.

Scooter stood behind the bar, pouring bourbon into multiple glasses.

"I'm fine," she said, before Savage could speak. "It's just a graze."

He didn't contradict her, just sat in a vacant chair. Joel immediately got up and disappeared into the back office, taking the medical kit with him.

"Any idea who did this?" he asked.

She arched an eyebrow. "Who'd you think?"

"Axle?"

A firm nod. "That would be my guess. Fucking chickenshit. Too scared to show his face. Took a shot at me from across the road."

"Any witnesses?"

"Joel saw the muzzle flash. Shooter was parked off the highway, behind the tree line."

"He was in a car?"

"No, a dirty brown pickup. Probably stolen."

"Get a plate?" he asked Joel, as the biker came back into the bar.

"Nah, too far away."

Savage gave a frustrated nod. That didn't help.

Scooter stalked over and set four glasses of bourbon on the table. Savage glanced up, surprised, but the VP just shrugged and sat down.

The others downed theirs. Savage left his on the table, untouched.

"You want protection?" he asked, although the marshals should already be providing it.

64

DUST DEVIL

"I've already got a tail," she hissed. "Although fuck knows where they were when it came down to it."

Good point.

"They weren't around?"

"Came running after the fact. Heard the shot and came to check it out. Bloody useless. Axle still got within shooting distance right under their noses."

"Where are they now?" he asked.

She shrugged. "Who knows?"

Savage hadn't seen the marshals' cruiser outside when he'd arrived. "Okay, I'll follow up with them."

"I don't need a babysitter, Sheriff. I need him put back behind bars."

"Until that happens, you're still a target," he said, grimly. "If Axle's out to get you, you can bet he'll try again. Better they're around than not."

She snorted. "For all the good it'll do."

IT WAS close to midnight when Savage finally headed home. The earlier sunset had long since given way to darkness, but the horizon still smoldered with the faint orange glow of distant flames. As he neared the turnoff for his place, a pair of headlights appeared in his rearview mirror. He squinted, trying to gauge the distance.

Close.

Getting closer.

His hand slid to the pistol resting beside him.

No one came out this way unless they had a reason. Apple Tree Farm was on an isolated stretch of road. There was nothing out here but brush and scrubland.

He eased off the gas. The car behind slowed too.

His pulse ticked higher.

Just before the turnoff to his place, the vehicle overtook his Suburban and disappeared behind the rise.

65

Savage exhaled. Maybe he'd imagined it.

It had been a long day, and his nerves were shot.

He kept going, tires crunching over gravel until he pulled up outside his farmhouse. He cut the engine, stepped out, and scanned the darkness, listening. All he could hear were crickets against the wind.

No car, and no engine. Still, the hairs on the back of his neck hadn't settled.

He walked toward his porch, muscles aching. It could've been nothing.

Then again, it could have been Axle.

If he'd already taken a shot at Rosalie, and failed, it made sense he'd come gunning for the other person who'd put him away.

Savage opened the door, walked inside, and rubbed a hand over his stubbly jaw. His eyes were gritty and dry as he stared into the darkness. Before doing anything else, he reached for the shotgun.

If Axle Weston was coming for him, he'd just have to make sure he was prepared.

ELEVEN

SLEEP DIDN'T COME EASY.

Every creak in the old farmhouse sounded louder and more ominous than usual. Every distant bark of a coyote, every gust of wind against the windowpane made Savage sit up on high alert.

The shotgun stood propped against his nightstand, his pistol on the pillow beside him where Becca used to be. He scoffed at the irony. Choices. It all boiled down to choices, and he'd chosen the job.

He thought of those taillights disappearing over the rise on the Durango Road and felt the hairs on his arms prickle.

Damn Axle Weston.

Still, it could've been nothing.

Then again, it could've been a warning.

His thoughts turned back to Becca, and his chest tightened.

He missed her voice.

She used to calm him in a way nobody else ever could. The evenings when the weight of the badge sat too heavy, she'd smile at him and ask if he wanted to talk about it. She'd offer some insight, some glimpse into the criminal mind that would help him work thorough a problem or hit on a solution. But not anymore.

He'd let her down, he knew that. But damn it, she'd known who he was when they met. Long before they'd even got together. He'd been her patient before her lover.

Becca, of all people, knew what he'd dealt with in Denver. Knew of his demons, and she'd helped him get over them. Except, she hadn't been able to deal with the man he'd become.

Then Connor was born and everything shifted. Suddenly his job became a liability, and his enemies knew his family was his weak spot. Danger had come to their door more times than he'd care to admit. Because of him. Because of the job.

Like tonight.

This was exactly why she'd left—and he couldn't blame her.

She needed more. Connor needed more. They deserved more.

It didn't make him miss them any less, though.

Before he could stop himself, he reached for his phone and video-called her. It was late, but maybe she was up, with Connor.

To his relief, Becca answered, her face tired but beautiful, framed by loose strands of auburn hair. She was in bed too, in the small rental place in Pagosa Springs.

"Hey," she said softly.

"Hey."

There was a pause, then Connor appeared, climbing into her lap. Becca gave a tired laugh. "He's not sleepy."

"Hi, buddy," he said, breaking into a smile.

Connor beamed and reached for the phone, and Savage felt a swell of emotion.

"Look at you. Such a big boy." He glanced at Becca. "I swear he's bigger than when you left."

"He is." She brushed a hand through Connor's curls. "He's getting so heavy."

Savage's eyes met hers. "How are you holding up?"

"I'm exhausted," she said honestly. "But we're okay."

"You could come home," he offered quietly. "It's gotta be better than being alone."

Becca's expression changed, tightening. "I can't, Dalton. I can't worry about you and take care of Connor. I can't wonder if every car that passes is going to run me off the road or every stranger in the playground is going to kidnap our son. I can't keep looking over my shoulder, it's too much."

Like now.

He didn't argue. He couldn't. She wasn't wrong.

"You know I never meant for it to turn out like this," he muttered.

"I know," she whispered. "Neither did I."

He swallowed hard over the lump in his throat. "I miss you."

She didn't respond.

"Take care of him for me," he added.

"I always do."

They ended the call with quiet goodbyes. Civil. Even cordial. But there was an edge to her voice now like she was holding back her anger and disappointment.

She wasn't the only one.

Eventually, he fell into an uneasy sleep.

"YOU LOOK LIKE HELL," Barb remarked when he walked into the office the next morning.

"Thanks," he muttered, going straight to the kitchenette and pouring himself a cup of coffee. Hell was an understatement.

"You not sleeping?" she asked, following him in.

"I'm fine," he said, hoping to pacify her.

It didn't work.

"You're working too hard," she said, her voice gentle. "Why don't you take a few days and go down to Pagosa Springs?"

"I will when this is over," he said, striding past her to his office.

He'd just closed the door and sunk into his chair when there was a knock. Lucas poked his head inside. "Thought you might like an update. I called Houston PD and they're sending a unit to check on Diesel's mom. I tried speaking with her, but she sounded totally out of it. Slurring her words, not making much sense. Think she's high or drunk. Maybe both."

Savage grunted. "No wonder Diesel joined the Crimson Angels."

"From what I could make out, she didn't know about Honey Granger," Lucas went on. "The Houston officers will confirm once they speak with her."

Lucas had only just left when Sinclair appeared carrying a thin manilla folder. "Got the autopsy report from Ray."

Savage straightened. "Anything new?"

"No, just confirmed what we already know. The close-range gunshot wound to the head strongly indicates he was dead before he entered the water."

"So he was killed somewhere else, and his body dumped in the lake?"

"Looks like it. Ballistics confirm the slug was from a 9mm, possibly a Beretta or Glock. Nothing unique, but Ray said the bullet was unusually clean. It didn't shatter."

"Professional shot," Savage mused.

"Or someone who'd done it before," Sinclair concluded.

Sinclair hadn't left yet when Barb stuck her head through the doorway. "Dalton, you'll want to take this call."

He picked up the receiver. "Savage."

"This is Deputy Hayes from the Durango Sheriff's Department. Shelby told me to give you a call," came the voice. "We've found a body out by Tenmile Ridge."

Savage's stomach dropped. "Go on."

"Some kids found it in the old quarry. There's a Harley Davidson motorcycle nearby too—a low rider with cream fenders."

Savage's blood ran cold. That was Rosalie's bike.

"You sure?"

"Absolutely. I'm looking at it right now."

He sucked in a breath. Had Axle finally gotten to Rosalie? Had he taken her out?

"The body—is it a white female with long, black hair, around forty-five years old?"

"Negative. It's a man. AFIS confirms ID is Axle Weston."

Savage closed his eyes for a moment, the tension draining from his shoulders.

Thank God.

"What?" mouthed Sinclair.

He covered the phone with his hand. "We can tell the marshals the manhunt is over."

Sinclair blinked. "Wait—Axle's dead?"

Savage gave a tight nod. "Yep, someone beat them to it."

TWELVE

THE SUN HADN'T CLEARED the trees when Savage and Sinclair pulled up to the old quarry off Tenmile Road. Out here, they could see first-hand how the drought had stripped the land bare. Everything looked sun-bleached and brittle. To make matters worse, a low haze clung to the tree line, thanks to the wind blowing smoke over from the still-burning wildfires.

Deputy Hayes met them at the perimeter near a weathered gate that had long since rusted off its hinges. He pointed up the incline toward the rim of the quarry. "Body's over there, about thirty yards in."

Savage and Sinclair followed the narrow trail, boots scraping over dry rock and dirt. The quarry opened up like a shallow wound in the earth, its gravel floor scattered with weeds and broken machinery. A few faded beer cans and cigarette butts hinted that local teens still used it for parties, although it was deserted now.

The body lay slumped beside a boulder at the edge of the drop, a dark pool soaked into the dirt beneath it. Savage immediately spotted Rosalie's motorcycle standing nearby, coated in dust. As the

DUST DEVIL

deputy had said, it was a low rider with cream fenders and a custom exhaust.

Sinclair crouched beside it. "You sure this is Rosalie's bike?"

Savage gave a grim nod. "Yeah, a hundred percent."

Sinclair blew out a breath. "So, what the hell's it doing here?"

Savage stared down at the body of Axle Weston. In his late forties, with a graying beard, he looked strangely composed in death. Calmer than he ever had in life. His leather jacket was open at the front, a massive blood stain seeping through his dirty white T-shirt.

"Maybe Axle rode it," he muttered.

"Or she gave him a ride out here," Sinclair suggested.

Savage bent down for a closer look.

"Looks like he was shot," Sinclair said, standing back.

Savage gave a slow nod. "Twice. There are two holes in his chest."

Sinclair pulled out her phone and took some preliminary photographs. "You think this was an execution too? Close range?"

He shrugged. "Not sure. One shot is dead center, but the other is on the right side, above the ribs. I wouldn't say this was a professional."

"An altercation, then?" she asked.

Savage straightened when he heard the sound of tires crunching over gravel.

Thanks to Barb's quick thinking, Pearl and Ray arrived, having set off at almost the same time as them.

Savage stood over Axle's body, waving away the flies, as they walked up the dusty path toward the quarry. Both were kitted up in their forensic gear.

"Morning, Sheriff. Sinclair," Pearl said.

They both nodded a greeting.

Ray gave him a once over. "You look like hell."

He grimaced. "So I've heard."

The ME turned his attention to the body. "At least this one's recent."

73

Savage knew what he meant. They'd be able to glean a lot more from Axle's body than they had Diesel's. Time was not their friend when it came to human remains.

"Another biker?"

Savage nodded. "An escaped fugitive, actually. You'd better be quick, we'll have the U.S. Marshals Service out here soon." He didn't want them taking Axle's body away when it was his homicide case. Now Axle was no longer wanted, it fell to his jurisdiction, and since it could be connected to Diesel's murder, he didn't want to go through a bunch of red tape to get the information he needed.

Ray got straight to work. Savage waited with Sinclair, surveying the area, looking for anything that could prove Rosalie had been here along with her ex-husband. No obvious boot prints, but then the ground was too hard and compact for that.

"I don't see any other bike tracks." Sinclair surveyed the ground around where the Harley stood.

"There are several tire tracks in the lot," Pearl pointed out. "Hard to tell which are recent, though. Place is so damn dry. I'll take photographs on my way back, just in case."

"Thanks, Pearl."

Tire tracks were useless by themselves, but might help them later on, when they had something to match them to.

"You think she did it?" Sinclair turned to him.

"I hope not." But he had to admit, it wasn't looking good.

Ray cleared his throat.

Savage refocused on the ME. "What you got?"

"Blood's pooled underneath the victim, and judging by the lividity, I'd say he hasn't been moved."

"So he was shot out here," Savage concluded.

Ray nodded. "Two gunshot wounds, both in the upper torso. I think I can say with reasonable certainty it was the center shot that killed him. Straight through the heart, severed the aorta."

Savage gave a somber nod. "He was shot standing up and dropped where he fell?"

"Yeah, that would be my guess," Ray confirmed.

"Any idea of the time of death?" Sinclair asked.

Ray pursed his lips. "Going by the lividity and rigor, at least twelve hours. So last night, in the hours before midnight. We'll know more after the autopsy."

Savage nodded, jaw tight. He had so many questions. "If Rosalie shot him, why bring him out here on her own motorcycle, and then leave it here? It doesn't make sense."

"She could have shot him then hitched a ride back with Scooter, or someone else," Sinclair suggested.

Savage frowned. He wasn't sure about that. "Either way, we have to speak to her."

"You want me to get Lucas to bring her in?" Sinclair asked.

Savage nodded. Rosalie wasn't going to like it, but Axle's death changed things. Right now, she was the primary suspect in her ex-husband's murder, and she'd better have a damn good alibi, otherwise it would be hard to prove she didn't do it.

BY THE TIME Savage got back to the station, the sun was higher in the cobalt blue sky and the air even thicker with smoke. He wiped his brow with his sleeve, drank some bottled water, then went to face Rosalie, who waited for him in an interview room.

As expected, she was not happy.

Lucas had tested her hands and clothing for gunshot residue but found nothing. That was something, at least.

Seated at the metal table, arms crossed, her expression was as cold as he'd ever seen it. Tension bent her shoulders inward, and she rubbed at her bandaged arm where Axle's bullet had grazed her.

She glanced up as he walked in. "What the hell is this, Dalton? Why'd you send your rookie to drag me out of my own bar?"

He shut the door behind him, then walked over to the table and took a seat. "Because your ex-husband was found dead this morning."

Her mouth fell open. "What?"

"Yep, we found him at the quarry. He'd been shot twice in the chest."

She sucked in a breath. "Jesus."

He frowned at her. "Rosalie, your motorcycle was left at the scene."

She stared at him, blood draining from her face. He had to admit, her surprise seemed real. "Mine?"

"Yeah. How do you account for that?" He folded his arms and studied her, assessing her reaction.

Her expression tightened. "It was stolen last night. I should have known that bastard took it."

"I take it by that bastard, you mean Axle?"

She nodded, distracted.

"Rosalie, this looks really bad for you. If you know anything, you'd better start talking."

"I don't know anything other than what I've already told you," she said, her eyes narrowing. "I heard the sound of a motorcycle during the night, so I ran outside, only to see someone take off on my bike. They forced the garage door."

"You didn't think to report it stolen?"

"I was going to. I just hadn't gotten around to it yet."

It was Savage's turn to slant his eyes. "You were going to?"

"Yeah, of course. I need a reference number for the insurance company. Maybe we can do that now?"

He ignored her question and stuck to the topic at hand. She could file her report later, once they were done here. "Okay, did you see Axle steal it?"

"No, but he's the only person we know who needs a ride," she shot back. "It's pretty damn obvious, don't you think?"

He had to admit, it was the most likely scenario. "Someone could have stolen it for him. Rourke or Skully, for example?"

She smirked. "They're back in the fold. No way they'd help him now."

He studied her. "Smart move, protecting them like that. You effectively bought their loyalty."

Her eyes gleamed. "That's how I know it wasn't them."

Fair enough. "You didn't see anything else?"

"No, but Axle knows how to get into the garage. He knows where I keep my spare set of keys. It would have been easy for him to take it."

"You didn't think to put measures in place in case this happened?"

She scowled at him. "I've got a damn U.S. Marshal cop car following me around. How was I supposed to know Axle would break into my place and steal my Harley?"

Good point.

Speaking of the marshals. "They were there last night?"

She gave a rough nod. "Yeah, for part of it, but when I went outside later, there was no sign of them. Useless idiots."

Savage frowned. He'd have to take that up with Randall.

"I don't suppose there was anyone with you last night?"

She stared at him, gaze hardening. "Why'd you ask?"

"Alibi. You can see how this looks. They're going to say you were helping your ex-husband escape and the two of you took a ride out to the quarry where you pulled a gun on him and got rid of him once and for all."

"Who's they? The marshals?"

"Yeah, or the jury at your trial."

A flicker of uncertainty marred her features. "That's ridiculous."

He shrugged, but he could tell she was rattled.

"Why the hell would I shoot him and leave my bike at the scene?" she asked. "I'm not stupid. Besides, how would I have gotten back into town?"

"You could have called someone to pick you up."

"Check my phone records."

He shot her a look. "We will, but you know as well as I do that we don't have your numerous burner numbers."

She smirked. "Makes it difficult to prove then, doesn't it?"

"Makes it difficult to disprove, too."

Her smile vanished. She leaned forward, placing her elbows on the table. "Dalton, you know I didn't do this?"

"Do I?"

She huffed. "Okay fine. If you think I shot the bastard, arrest me now."

He didn't move.

She raised her hands. "No gunshot residue. You've got nothing."

"Not yet."

Rosalie got to her feet. "Then you can't hold me."

"Sit down, Rosalie," he growled, beginning to lose his temper.

She stared at him for a long moment, then slowly sank back into the chair.

Savage continued, "I'm not the only one who wants to talk to you."

She shook her head. "Not those idiots?"

He shrugged. "Axle was their target."

"Jesus Christ. I swear that man is tormenting me from the grave."

He snorted.

Rosalie leaned back, crossed her slender arms, then winced and uncrossed them again. He saw a butterfly tattoo on the inside of her wrist that he hadn't noticed before.

"New tat?"

A shrug.

"It's nice. Suits you."

She gave a little shake of her head. "Go. Do your verifying and let me know when I can get the hell out of here. I've got stuff to do."

He resisted a smirk. She knew he was buying time to check out her phone records, any CCTV in the area, and follow up with the marshals. Nope, she wasn't stupid. That was for sure.

He got up, walked to the door and banged on it. Lucas, who was waiting outside, opened it. Before he left, Savage turned his head.

"You'd better hope I don't find anything, Rosalie, because this doesn't look good for you."

Her voice was grim. "Wouldn't Axle just love it if I went down for his murder? It would be like a final *screw you*."

"Let's hope that doesn't happen."

She just snorted and stared angrily at the wall.

THIRTEEN

"SHE'S NOT GOING ANYWHERE," Savage said. He sat opposite Randall in his office, elbows planted on the desk, staring the U.S. Marshall down.

"This is our jurisdiction," Randall argued. "And she's our prime suspect."

"No," Savage corrected coolly. "Axle Weston *was* your jurisdiction, but you let him get away when he stole Rosalie Weston's Harley-Davidson right in front of you."

The man's jaw tightened. "You don't know that was him."

"Well, whoever stole it did it right under your noses. What happened?"

Randall sighed. "My guys had a shift change. There was maybe fifteen minutes where her house did not have eyes on it."

Fifteen minutes in which Axle, who'd obviously been watching the property, took the opportunity to break into the garage, steal Rosalie's motorcycle and take off unseen.

But why had he headed out to the quarry?

"I want to take the wife in," Randall said.

"Sorry, no can do. This is a local homicide. It happened in my

80

county and on my soil. It's a murder investigation, not a fugitive recovery. Hawk's Landing Sheriff's Office has jurisdiction. You know it, and so will the D.A."

Randall's mouth twisted, clearly hating it. "Weston was ours. If the wife had a hand in it—"

"Ex-wife," he corrected. "And if she had a hand in it, we will investigate and charge her accordingly. You'll get your say if it turns federal. Until then, she stays here."

Randall gave an exaggerated sigh, dramatic enough to make Savage want to throttle him, but the marshal knew he'd been boxed in. State law gave Savage twenty-four hours to hold a homicide suspect without formal charges, and Randall couldn't override that.

"Fine," Randall muttered.

"Good." Savage stood, signaling the conversation was over. "My deputy will escort you to the interview room. You can question her here, under our supervision."

Randall pushed back his chair and stood stiffly. "Then let's not waste any more time."

THE MARSHAL LEFT after a full hour spent grilling Rosalie. She'd answered stoically, giving only necessary answers and never elaborating. Savage had to admire her grit. Then again, this wasn't her first experience with law enforcement.

Now, however, she stood behind the booking desk, tapping her fingers impatiently.

"You've got no cause to hold me, Dalton," she said sharply. "Either charge me or cut me loose."

"You should be grateful I held you here," Savage replied as Thorpe printed off her release paperwork. "If I'd let you go earlier, Randall would've hauled you to Albuquerque for federal processing. You'd still be sitting in a lockup by midnight, probably without bail."

She snorted. "Sure, Sheriff. Thanks for the hospitality."

He shook his head, watching as Thorpe handed her a clipboard.

She signed it without reading it and then sauntered out, her knee-high boots clacking down the steps to the street.

"That woman is trouble," Sinclair grumbled.

"You're not wrong," Savage said as a metallic growl made them both glance out the window. Scooter pulled up outside the office and Rosalie straddled the back of his motorcycle, wrapped her arms around his waist, and off they went.

They'd scarcely disappeared from sight when Barbara called, "Dalton, Ray is on Line One."

"Thanks, Barb. I'll take it in my office."

Savage headed to his office, sat down at his desk, and picked up the phone.

"Hey, Ray. You got something for me?" He was still awaiting the ballistics report on the gun that killed Axle, the forensic report, and of course, the autopsy, which, with a bit of luck, Ray had already completed. There wasn't much of a backlog in Hawk's Landing, and using the local couple meant he didn't have to wait in line for the bigger centers.

"Yeah, a couple of things," Ray replied. "Based on the wound tracks and lack of powder residue, your victim was shot from about six feet away. Three rounds fired. One missed, two hit."

"How do you know one missed?" Savage asked.

"Pearl recovered three shell casings at the scene but there were only two entry wounds."

"Three?" Shit, both he and Sinclair had missed that.

"Yeah, Pearl found a spent slug embedded in the quarry wall about two hundred yards off."

Savage scratched his head. So, the shooter was a bad shot? Or just desperate? Maybe Axle was moving, making him harder to hit.

"Go on."

"One shot entered an inch below the left clavicle, missing any vital organs. It would have hurt and caused internal trauma but wouldn't have killed him. The fatal shot was straight through the heart, as I said. From the trajectory, we think Weston was down on the ground when the kill shot was fired."

Savage exhaled. "So the first shot dropped him, and the second shot finished him off?"

"Yeah, that would be my call."

"Okay, gotcha. What about the motorcycle?"

"Hang on, let me pass you over to Pearl." There was a rustle as the phone changed hands. Pearl's voice came on. "Hey, Dalton."

"Hey, Pearl. What'd you find?"

"Rosalie Weston's DNA is all over the Harley-Davidson. Handlebars, seat, gas tank, foot pegs. Normal stuff you'd expect from someone who rides it regularly."

Savage grunted. No surprises there.

"As a result of the transfer, trace elements of her DNA were found on Axle Weston's clothing, particularly his jeans and gloves."

"So he was driving it?"

"Well, he was on it. Whether he was actually driving or not, I couldn't tell you."

Okay, that was something, although it didn't help Rosalie's case. "Anything else?"

"Yeah, and you'll be pleased about this."

"Oh?"

"The rounds we pulled from Weston match an older shooting case."

Savage sat up straighter. "They did? Ballistics found a match?"

"Yes."

Finally. He felt like fist-pumping the air.

It meant they might be able to trace the weapon to its owner and find out who the hell shot Axle Weston.

"This is right up your alley too," Pearl continued. "The shooting took place in Denver back in 2012. It was a police-involved shooting, actually, although it was ruled legit."

A cold chill trickled over him.

"Who was the cop?"

"Detective Zebadiah Swift shot and killed a fugitive in a parking lot outside a mall in Downtown Denver."

The bottom dropped out of his stomach. He sat there, staring at the wall as Pearl's words ricocheted through his head.

What the hell?

It couldn't be.

"Dalton, you there?" Pearl enquired.

"Yeah." He scraped his thoughts together.

"It was a department-issued service pistol. That should narrow down your search."

"It's... not what I was expecting," he croaked.

She chuckled. "Never is. People continue to shock the hell out of me. At least the evidence never lies."

"You sure about that?" He gripped the phone like his life depended on it. "About the gun, I mean."

"Of course. It was the same gun, same barrel markings. No mistake."

Goddammit.

"Thanks, Pearl. Gotta go." Reeling, he hung up.

He was familiar with the parking lot incident. Way too familiar. That was when he'd nearly lost his life trying to protect a pregnant woman.

Closing his eyes, he remembered lying there on the hard tarmac, his body covering hers, his partner bleeding out beside him, certain the next shot would end it all.

Then fate had stepped in—or rather, Zeb had—and taken out the assailant.

He'd saved his life.

FOURTEEN

"YOU OKAY, BOSS?" Thorpe asked as Savage walked out of his office. His head spun as he tried to process what he'd learned.

"We need to look into Zebediah Swift's records," he said, giving it a quick shake. It didn't work. He still felt like he was in a daze. "Bank details, phone data, anything that might link him to Axle Weston or Diesel Vaugn, our first victim."

Sinclair's eyebrows shot up. "You like Zeb for this?"

He swallowed hard. "I just found out it was his gun that killed Axle."

Sinclair gave a low whistle.

"Yeah, I know. I'm going to bring him in for questioning."

"Want me to pick him up?" Lucas offered.

"Nah, I've got to do it. We've got history."

Lucas glanced at Sinclair, who gave a little shake of her head.

"Sure thing." Lucas turned back to his screen.

"Want some company?" Sinclair asked.

"Nope. I can manage Zeb on my own."

She gave a nod, but he could see she had questions. They all did.

Sure enough, Sinclair's curiosity got the better of her. "Why would Zeb take out Axle Weston? He didn't have an issue with him."

"That we know of," Thorpe pointed out, mid swivel.

"That's what we need to find out," Savage said. "See what you can dig up by the time I get back. If there's a connection between them, we need to find it."

She gave a sympathetic nod. Both Sinclair and Thorpe were aware of his tumultuous past relationship with Zeb.

———

ALL SAVAGE COULD THINK about on the way to the Hidden Gem Trailer Park was that day. He relived the events like a movie on a loop.

"FREEZE, *put your hands above your head!*"

The fugitive running, the gunshots ringing out, his partner falling to the ground.

A pregnant woman screaming, dropping her shopping bags.

Another shot—it went wide.

He pulled the woman down and shielded her body with his own.

The fugitive jumped into a nearby vehicle. The window slid down and a gun appeared.

Aimed at them.

"Don't shoot!" he yelled.

The man fired—it hit the asphalt inches from them. Another shot and his partner cried out, clutching his leg.

He was bleeding out.

The fugitive twisted in his seat and took aim. This time he had a better angle. This time it would be game over.

A crack as the weapon discharged. Savage squeezed his eyes shut.

Still breathing.

He opened them to find the fugitive slumped over the steering wheel, a spray of red mist coating the windshield in front of him.

What the hell had just happened?

How'd the shooter end up dead?

Zeb appeared, holding his gun at the ready.

"You okay?"

"I am, but my partner's not."

The man wasn't moving.

Then came the ambulance... the tears, the thanks.

"Just glad I could be there," Zeb said.

ZEB HAD HANDED his weapon over to Internal Affairs. He'd had to. Standard protocol. The shoot had to be recorded. The slug entered into the system.

Only to pop up again now, over a decade later.

Savage shook his head.

What were the chances?

THE TRAILER PARK entrance loomed ahead, a shadowy gap between rows of majestic pines. Savage turned in, his tires crunching over the dip, kicking up dust. He cruised down the gravel road, mindful of the kids, stray dogs, potheads, and drunks that roamed around here, until he got to Zeb's place.

Getting out of the Suburban, he heard voices from behind the mobile home. Circling around the side of the property, he came across Zeb, three scantily dressed women, and two bikers sitting around a firepit, beers in hand.

"Bit early, isn't it?" Savage nodded at the drinks.

A young woman smoking a joint coughed and tried to hide it behind her back. He ignored her. "Zeb, can I have a word?"

The former detective glared at him. "Really? Now?"

"Yeah." His tone didn't leave room for debate. Zeb must've

clocked it too, because he stood up, set his drink on the edge of the firepit, and said, "Let's go inside."

"What's this about?" Zeb asked, once they were in the kitchen. The window framed the wall of fir trees rising beyond the back lot. The sun speckled the grass with restless patterns. It was pretty, but Savage was too distracted to appreciate it.

"Look, man. I'm sorry to have to do this, but I need to bring you in for questioning. You can come voluntarily, or I can cuff you. Up to you."

"What the hell?" Zeb sputtered. "Why?"

"Axle Weston was found dead yesterday. He'd been shot." Savage gave him the basic courtesy.

"Axle? Jesus." Zeb ripped off his baseball cap and ran a hand through his thinning hair. "Sorry to hear that, but what's it gotta do with me?"

Savage watched him closely. If Zeb was guilty, he was hiding it well. His confusion looked real.

"Well, there's the rub, Zeb." Savage took a breath. "He was shot with your gun."

The outburst was expected.

"What the f—?" Before Zeb could finish, Savage had whipped the cuffs from his belt, snapped them on, and secured them behind Zeb's back. He wasn't taking any chances with the ex-cop.

"I warned you," he muttered.

"Hell, man, you know me! I wouldn't kill Axle. What the fuck for?"

"That's what we need to find out." Savage led him toward the front door. He had no intention of trailing a handcuffed Zeb past the inebriated bikers and stoned women. Luckily, Zeb seemed relatively sober. Just to be safe, he'd leave him to dry out for a couple of hours before he questioned him.

"You arresting me?" Zeb asked, as Savage secured him in the back of the Suburban.

"Not unless you want me to," Savage retorted.

"I swear, I didn't do this."

"Save it for questioning. You know the drill. You're entitled to an attorney, if you want one."

"I got nothing to hide," Zeb muttered, but Savage knew better. Every seasoned cop knew the importance of having a lawyer in that room, innocent or guilty.

Sure enough, back at the Sheriff's office, Zeb asked for counsel. Savage made sure Thorpe documented Zeb's request on the custody log to avoid any future legal headaches.

"This will be strictly by the book," Savage said to Sinclair, who stood at the desk, watching the proceedings.

The interview was set for 5 p.m., after the alcohol had a chance to wear off. He wasn't going to give Zeb an impaired judgment excuse. The lawyer, Kurt Fisher, arrived—an awkward beanpole of a man wearing a tight-fitting suit and wire-framed glasses.

Savage gave them five minutes of private consultation time, which was standard under Miranda and local policy, before entering Interview Room One. As usual, the conversation would be recorded on both audio and video, plus monitored live from the observation room.

After formal introductions had taken place, Savage slid a crime scene photo of Axle Weston across the table. Zeb glanced down at it with a practiced eye.

The victim's eyes were closed, but the two bullet holes in his chest stained his shirt brown. There was a dried pool of dirt beneath him too, and dust coated his clothes, his hair and his boots.

The setup was not new to Zeb, but he was used to being on the other side of the table. Still, Savage dispensed with the games, since Zeb would see them coming a mile away.

Instead, he opted for a straightforward approach.

Cop to cop.

"The two bullets we pulled from the victim's body matched a gun registered to you back in 2012. It was your service pistol—the one you kept after you left the Force," Savage said, watching Zeb's face.

89

His eyes widened slightly, but his mouth stayed stiff. When he spoke, it was a low growl. "I haven't had that gun in years. I bought it when I retired, but it was stolen."

"Stolen?" How convenient. "When was this?"

"Years ago. One of my girls took it for protection without my knowledge. It got taken out of the trailer."

"You left your gun lying around for anyone to take?" Savage slanted his gaze at him. He'd have to do better than that.

The lawyer leaned over, presumably to tell Zeb he didn't have to answer that. Zeb waved him away. "No, course not, but she knew where I kept it. All the girls did, just in case there was ever a problem."

Savage supposed when you ran an illegal brothel, there were often 'problems.'

"Why didn't you report the theft?"

"I was hoping it'd turn up."

"Sure you were."

The lawyer didn't comment. They both knew the reason Zeb hadn't reported it was because he'd have to explain how it went missing, which would mean admitting he ran girls out of the trailer park. That could have caused all kinds of complications.

"When exactly did it go missing?" Savage asked.

Zeb scratched his head. "You know, I can't remember exactly. Maybe three or four years ago."

"Before Diesel vanished?"

Zeb hesitated, and he glanced at his lawyer who gave a teeny shake of his head. "Don't recall."

"Would your girls remember?" Savage asked. Maybe if Zeb thought he was going to bring them in, he'd offer up the information. Any hint of an arrest was bad for business.

"I think it was after he disappeared."

"Right."

Was he lying? Savage couldn't tell, and he'd probably never

know. Unfortunately, there was no way of finding out. "Can you give me the name of the person who took it?"

"Her name was Noel. I don't know if that was her real name. She isn't with me anymore."

Savage swore under his breath. Typical Zeb. Another dead end. Then again, this wasn't the former cop's first rodeo. He knew how to play the system, having spent most of his working life on the other side of it.

"Got an address for her? A contact number?"

"Nope. Never did. Most of these girls come to me desperate for work. I don't ask questions, and they don't tell me their stories. None of my business, anyway. All I care about is they're clean and want to work."

Frustration seethed inside of him. "Okay, just so I've got this straight. Your explanation is someone used your gun, which was stolen several years ago, to kill Axle Weston, a fugitive and former president of an outlaw motorcycle club that you belong to?"

Zeb gave a cocky grin. "That about sums it up, yeah."

Shit.

Savage changed tack. "Where were you last night between eight o'clock and midnight?"

"I was at the Roadhouse."

"You know my next question."

"Can anyone vouch for me? Only a bar full of bikers, although I grant you, they're not the most reliable of witnesses." He chuckled, before his face hardened. "I got home after twelve, as I'm sure my neighbors will confirm, and didn't leave the house after that."

"We'll follow up." A Harley-Davison was not a quiet motorcycle. Everyone in that trailer park would have heard him come home.

Fisher cleared his throat. "If there are no further questions, my client would like to leave."

"That's it for now." Savage got to his feet.

The lawyer gave a tight nod.

"Thanks for coming in," Savage said to Zeb, an edge to his voice.

"No problem." Zeb gave an unconvincing shrug. "Sorry I couldn't be of more help."

Savage let Thorpe handle the release papers and went back to his office. He wanted to believe Zeb was telling the truth, but something about the theft of his service pistol didn't ring true.

It wasn't like the Denver cop to shoot anyone in cold blood. He may have been a corrupt police officer, but lifting drugs from evidence was a far cry from committing murder. Old habits die hard, and Savage knew it would take a lot for Zeb to take a life.

He sighed. Still, it had been known to happen.

One thing was for sure, he wouldn't get anything out of Zeb via official channels, but now that he had his statement on record, he could set about tearing it apart.

FIFTEEN

"IT GETS WORSE," Thorpe said, later that evening. It had been a long day, and the whole team was still at the office.

Savage could feel the grit behind his eyes and imagined the others could too. He poured himself yet another cup of coffee and stared at his deputy. "Tell me."

"Zeb's bank statements show several large cash deposits and corresponding withdrawals in the year preceding Diesel's death," Thorpe explained. "That activity isn't suspicious in itself, but get this, they stop after Diesel disappeared."

"You think they're related?" Sinclair asked, wearily. She looked exhausted, her normally bright eyes smudged with shadows. "Zeb depositing that money and then withdrawing it again might have nothing to do with Diesel."

She'd been on the phone to Mason throughout the afternoon getting updates on the wildfire situation. After a relatively calm night during which the wind had died down, it had sprung up again and pushed the fire ever closer to the evacuation zone. They had people staying at inns, hotels and resorts nearby, unable to return to their homes.

The sooner the fire was out, the better. It seemed just when Mason and his team thought they'd made headway, a stiff gust or scorching spark started it up again.

"Wish I'd known about this before we released him," Savage said, frowning. "Could have asked him about it."

"We can always pay him another visit," Sinclair suggested.

"Wouldn't be on the record though." Savage massaged his forehead. "Still, we might have to. How large were these deposits and withdrawals?"

"A couple thousand bucks each time," Thorpe told him. "The withdrawals are exactly half the deposited amount each time."

"Sounds like a contract," Sinclair murmured.

Lucas cleared his throat. "Zeb could have taken on some extra work. Maybe he pulled in the cash doing security jobs or something and then withdrew some of it afterwards. Doesn't mean it's connected to Diesel."

"You're right."

They shouldn't assume the money was from illegal activities, although knowing Zeb, that was the more likely source. They also shouldn't assume it was from something he was up to with Diesel. However, the fact that both the deposits and withdrawals had ceased once Diesel had died was a coincidence he couldn't ignore.

"Let's not forget Diesel was an outlaw biker," Sinclair countered. "He was trusted muscle, used to running illegal errands for the MC."

Thorpe leaned forward. "Maybe Diesel and Zeb had a little side hustle. If it had something to do with the Angels, Rosalie might know."

"Rosalie won't tell us anything." Savage knew that for a fact. The woman was tighter lipped than a fully-choked carburetor.

A wave of tiredness washed over him. They were all beat. He made a judgement call. "You know what? Let's call it a day. We can come back to this tomorrow with fresh heads. Zeb's not going anywhere."

There were several relieved nods of agreement. They weren't going to make any headway tonight. Not like this.

THE NEXT MORNING, Savage was halfway through his second cup of coffee when Pearl called from the lab.

"Morning, Dalton. Time to get excited. I've got something interesting for you."

Please let that be true.

After another torturous night's sleep, he needed some good news.

"Give it to me." He reached for his pen.

"You remember that old piece of leather Diesel had with him when his body was found? Looked like a worn strip?"

"Yeah?"

"Well, we ran a deeper scan on the lining. First an X-ray and then chemical tests. Turns out, there was a faint residue inside."

"What was it?"

He heard Pearl grin. "Cocaine."

Savage straightened up, the weariness vanishing in a breath. "You're telling me Diesel was transporting drugs?"

"Sure looks that way. Not for personal use either. For trace residue to be found after all this time, it would suggest a large quantity or multiple shipments."

"Don't suppose you found any prints?"

"Sadly, no. Not after being submerged under water for so long."

After jotting down a few more details, Savage thanked Pearl and hung up. Then he strode out of his office and into the bullpen, a definite spring in his step.

They all looked up expectantly.

"Okay, listen up. We now know Diesel was a courier. Cocaine."

There were several surprised murmurs.

"For who?" Sinclair asked. "The MC?"

Savage considered this. "Maybe. But think about it—he died and the money in and out of Zeb's account stopped. Could be he was giving Zeb a cut, or—and this is the more likely scenario, in my opinion—Zeb was paying him for something."

Thorpe stroked his jaw contemplatively. "If Diesel was running drugs, and the money trail leads to Zeb—"

"Then Zeb was bankrolling him," Sinclair finished. "Not the club."

Thorpe nodded. "It makes sense. The cash withdrawals could have been payments to Diesel. Off the books. They're not consistent enough to be payroll, and they're too regular to be random."

"Exactly." Savage paced up and down as his head cleared. "Diesel was his mule. He moved the coke in his tool bag, while Zeb paid him cash to run it across state lines."

A horrible thought struck him. "Maybe Diesel got spooked or decided he wanted to stop to run away with Honey Granger."

"And he gets silenced," Thorpe finished. "Zeb couldn't risk the exposure."

Savage rubbed his jaw. "Shit."

He didn't want to believe it. Didn't want to believe Zeb was capable of that.

"It does make sense," Sinclair decided. "Diesel disappears, and the withdrawals stop."

"What about the deposits?" Savage turned to Thorpe. "What happened to them?"

Thorpe's mouth formed a grim line. "They stopped too."

SIXTEEN

THE DRIVE OUT to Hidden Gem was long enough for Savage to rehearse what he'd say—but not long enough to come up with anything that didn't end with his fist in Zeb's face. If their theory was true, the former cop had lied to him.

Lied to his face.

Savage didn't know exactly what the nature of Diesel and Zeb's relationship was, but he was damned sure going to find out.

The smoke from the wildfires clung to the hills. Everything around him felt like it was dying. Maybe that was just his current mood talking. He threw off the melancholy as he pulled onto the dried grass in front of Zeb's mobile home and killed the engine. Time to get to the bottom of this.

He got out of the Suburban and glanced around, but apart from a couple of kids playing on a broken swing set, there wasn't anyone about. A fly buzzed around his head, but he swatted it away.

Zeb's truck was parked outside, his Harley-Davidson next to it. Good, he was home. In the background, Savage heard music. A Blues guitar, low and melodic. He climbed the steps to the porch and knocked on the door.

97

L.T. RYAN

When nobody answered it, he tried the handle. To his surprise, it was unlocked.

"Zeb, it's Savage," he called.

He found Zeb at the kitchen table, drinking bourbon, a half-empty bottle on the table beside him.

Savage raised a hand. "Don't get up."

Zeb glared at him. "What the hell are you doing here? I've told you everything I know."

"Except you didn't, did you? You were lying to me."

Zeb frowned.

"I know you were using Diesel to move product."

"What? No!"

Maybe it was the booze, maybe he was just getting to know Zeb, but he could tell the guy was bullshitting. "We found evidence on Diesel that says otherwise."

"If he was carrying drugs, that's club business. Got nothing to do with me."

"Come on, Zeb. You were paying him, weren't you? We can see the money flowing in and out of your bank account in the months leading up to his murder."

Zeb's jaw tensed. "That proves zilch. You got it in for me, or something, Dalton? Why are you bringing this shit up now?"

"Because two men are dead, Zeb. I don't want to believe the worst of you, but you gotta give me something here. You can see how it looks."

"It's circumstantial, at best."

He wasn't wrong.

"True, but with your history—" He didn't need to finish. Zeb had been fired under allegations of corruption. He was lucky he'd got away without being prosecuted. If this went to trial, circumstantial might just be enough.

A long beat dragged out. Savage kept his gaze locked on Zeb's.

Eventually, the former cop threw up his hands. "Okay, okay. You win. Yeah, I asked Diesel to get rid of some stash for a friend."

DUST DEVIL

He fucking knew it.

Savage ran a hand through his hair. "Jesus, Zeb."

Zeb shrugged. "What? It was voluntary. Diesel wanted in. He said he needed the extra cash—for Honey. I needed a courier. We came to an arrangement."

Savage fixed his gaze on him. "By friend, you mean a dirty cop?"

Zeb stared at his glass. "Look, man. The guy had some product to sell, and I was helping him get rid of it. That's all."

"Let me guess, the coke was from a police lockup. Evidence confiscated in a bust?"

Zeb didn't reply.

Savage gave him a long look. "You still doing that shit?"

"Nah, it was a long time ago. I don't have any police contacts anymore." He reached for a pack of cigarettes and lit one.

Savage watched as the man inhaled deeply. "I could arrest you for distribution, conspiracy."

Zeb blew smoke at the ceiling. "No, you can't. Not now."

Savage tensed, knowing what was coming.

"Five years, Dalton. Statute of limitations on non-continuing distribution is five years. And this wasn't a continuing operation. It was one job. One time. Long ago."

"There are numerous payments."

"We broke it down into smaller packages to sell it. Couldn't offload the whole lot in one go. That would have been way too obvious."

Damn, he was right.

"I should take you in," Savage growled.

"You can't touch me. The product is long gone, as is the cash. My name never came up in the Denver bust. The guy who got pinched— my buddy—he rolled over and took the heat. Never even mentioned me."

"Did you testify?"

"Hell, no. Didn't need to. The case got buried. He pled out. End of story."

Savage's eyes narrowed. "Why Diesel?"

"We needed a runner," Zeb said. "Diesel was perfect. He did the same thing for the Angels, and this was a profitable sideline."

Savage put his hands on his hips. "What happened after Diesel disappeared?"

Zeb shrugged, confused. "Nothing, why?"

"The payments stopped."

"We'd got rid of all the product. There was no more to sell."

Savage stared at him. "You sure you didn't shoot Diesel to stop him talking? Maybe he wanted to go to Axle with this? Maybe he wanted out, but you didn't?"

He was theorizing here, hoping something would resonate.

Zeb stabbed out his cigarette. "I didn't kill him, Dalton. There was no reason to. We both made some money on the side and went our separate ways. Nobody else ever found out about it."

Savage gave him a hard look. "You sure about that?"

"Look, Axle didn't know about it. He'd have kicked off if he did. Trust me, that's not something he would have tolerated. Not without wanting a cut. Axle was a mean bastard."

That much he knew.

"What about Rosalie?"

"Rosalie was nothing in those days. Background noise, that's all."

That's what Zeb thought, but Savage knew better. Rosalie had been the one who'd held the club together. It was she who'd planned the heists, made the contacts and set up the jobs. Axle had thought he was in charge, but really, he'd always been her proxy. She'd played him like a fiddle—played them all.

Zeb smirked. "You can't touch me for what I did."

"Maybe, but I can ruin your life," Savage said quietly. "I can sit outside your mobile home with a patrol unit every night. I can dig through every girl you've ever hired, every under-the-table job you've taken, every dollar the IRS didn't see. You think I won't?"

Zeb's face tightened. "Why do that? I swear, I had nothing to do with Diesel's murder."

DUST DEVIL

Savage let out a frustrated breath. He knew when he was bested. There was no way of proving or disproving Zeb's story. No way of knowing whether Axle knew about the drug distribution. No way of knowing who had killed Diesel.

Maybe it was time he had another heart to heart with Rosalie. Despite what Zeb thought, Axle could have mentioned it to her.

Annoyed, he turned to leave.

Zeb called after him. "You want to know who killed Diesel, Dalton, you'll have to look someplace other than me."

Savage didn't stop walking.

SEVENTEEN

ROSALIE DROVE UP THE LONG, meandering drive to Apple Tree Farm, aware that the low, throaty growl of the loaner would announce her presence. After Savage had left that cryptic message on her phone, she'd decided to come and see him herself, rather than take a chance he'd turn up at her place again.

She couldn't have the goddamned sheriff stopping by like they were friends. That was not good for business.

She'd never been to Savage's home before. It was nice. She liked the wide-open space, the view of the open plains, the purple hue of the snow-covered mountain peaks in the distance. Like her place, it had that silent air of isolation that could be both lonely and peaceful at the same time.

In some ways, they were very alike.

As expected, he heard her coming and was waiting outside on the porch, shotgun in hand. Only when she removed her helmet, did he set it down beside the door.

"Rosalie? What are you doing here?" He glanced behind her down the drive as if he half-expected to see a posse of bikers trailing her.

"I'm alone," she said. Swinging her leg over, she dismounted. "Nobody knows I'm here."

He relaxed, his shoulders lowering. "You got my message?"

"Yeah."

He looked tired, five o'clock shadow tinting his square jaw, hazel eyes bruised with fatigue. She spread her arms. "You going to invite me in? I sure could use a drink."

He looked like he could too.

The property had a wide porch from which to admire the uninterrupted views. Two wicker chairs faced the mountain—except now, there was only one person to sit in them. She'd heard about Becca's departure. This was a small town and news travelled fast. Rumor was Savage's partner had up and left with the kid. Couldn't cut it being a Sheriff's wife. Too dangerous. Too lonely.

Rosalie had snorted when she'd heard. If Becca thought that was tough, she should try running a male-dominated, outlaw motorcycle club.

Savage gestured to the chairs. "Take a seat. I'll be right back."

Rosalie walked up the steps but didn't sit down. Instead, she turned and lifted her face toward the peaks. The air was warm, tinged with smoke, the sky deeper, the colors more intense than usual.

"That's caused by the wildfires," he said, coming back out.

She nodded. Smoke always made the sunset way more vivid.

"What's the current status?" she asked, taking the glass he offered.

"The fires are under control for now—but only just. If the wind picks up, or changes direction, we've got a problem."

"I heard you'd evacuated the houses on the ridge."

"Just a precaution." He glanced up at the sky. "What we really need is some rain."

She nodded distractedly, then turned to face him. It was time to get down to business. "What did you want to ask me?"

He hesitated, then eased his frame into a chair, stretching his long legs out in front of him. It creaked under his weight. After a moment's hesitation, she did the same.

"I wanted to talk about something Diesel was involved in, three years ago," he said, once she'd leaned back and crossed her legs.

Rosalie rolled her eyes. "Not this again. I told you, I wasn't part of that."

"But Axle talked to you. He told you everything."

She didn't deny it. Those were happier days, before everything went to shit. Before the cheating, the dangerous jobs, the recklessness. Axle had gotten power hungry, and it had affected his head. Made him rash.

Savage studied her in that intense way he had. "This didn't have anything to do with the club."

Rosalie frowned. Now he had her full attention. "What was it about, then?"

"A side deal. Freelance job—with Zeb."

"Zebadiah? The dirty cop?"

"That's the one. I think he and Diesel were smuggling coke into the county."

She blinked at him. "Behind Axle's back?"

Savage nodded. "I take it you didn't know about this?"

"Hell, no. And if I didn't, Axle didn't either."

"Maybe he just didn't tell you about it."

She considered this. Was it possible? Axle could be secretive, and they hadn't been open with each other for a few years before his arrest. He'd cut her off, sidelined her so he could squeeze her out.

"Maybe." Her voice was quiet. She didn't like to admit it, but it was possible. She glanced back at Savage. "Zeb tell you that?"

"Yeah."

She arched her eyebrows, surprised.

Savage gave an annoyed shrug. "Can't touch him for it. It's been too long."

"Ah." She gave a knowing nod. That made sense. Zeb was a crafty fox. He wouldn't have put himself on the line like that unless he knew he was safe. "Where'd he get the coke?"

"Not sure. Police lockup, most likely. A buddy needed to offload it, and Zeb saw the opportunity to make some extra cash. He said Diesel wanted in."

Rosalie pursed her lips. "Risky, keeping it from the club."

Savage frowned, leaning forwards. "You think Axle would have shot Diesel if he'd found out?"

Rosalie exhaled slowly. Would he?

"Maybe. Axle would have been mad, that's for sure. He'd have seen it as stealing from the club. A betrayal of his brothers. Something like that, you come to the club first. You don't use club resources and go behind their back for your own gain."

"Yet Zeb is still standing," Savage murmured, softly.

Rosalie saw where he was going with this. "You gotta ask yourself why. If Axle shot Diesel, surely he'd be gunning for Zeb too."

"Why not take him out three years ago?" Savage rubbed his jaw.

Rosalie stared at him. "Because we put him away before he could get to Zeb. You and me, Dalton."

Savage gave a slow nod. "Except, that changed when he busted out. They had unfinished business."

She hesitated, knowing they were both thinking the same thing. "Did Zeb shoot Axle?" Her voice dropped to a whisper. "Have we just cracked the case?"

Savage paused, drink in hand. The silence drew out, punctuated only by the crickets and cicadas, and the occasional hoot of an owl. Eventually, he said, "Zeb claims he didn't do it. Said he was at the Roadhouse that night."

Rosalie processed this, staring at the glass in her hand. Was he? She couldn't remember. Then she got it. This was the whole reason the Sheriff had contacted her to begin with.

Damn, he was good.

"You want to see the security camera footage from the bar the night Axle was killed."

105

The corners of his mouth tilted upwards, just a fraction. "If you'll show me, yeah."

She sighed, letting a long beat pass. "Okay, I'll see if I can find it."

His eyes lit up, and it struck her how handsome he was—in a rugged, grizzly kind of way. Didn't change the fact he'd manipulated her, however.

She downed her drink in one. "Well played, Dalton. I didn't see that one coming."

He smirked. "Thank you, Rosalie."

She stood up, handing him the empty glass. "I think it's time I hit the road."

Savage also got to his feet.

"Don't get used to this," she called over her shoulder as she strode toward her motorcycle.

"Evening visits?"

She gestured between them. "Me helping you. It's not going to become a regular thing."

"I know," he called after her.

She found she was smiling as she drove away.

EIGHTEEN

IT WAS mid-morning when Rosalie sent over the surveillance footage. Thorpe pulled it up, and Savage leaned over his shoulder as they fast-forwarded to the night of Axle's murder.

The angle was high and discreet. The camera perched above the bar, tucked in near the neon 'Bud' sign. Rosalie had once told Savage only she and Scooter knew it was there. Not even the other Angels were aware that they were being recorded.

"Insurance," she'd told him once. Given the clientele in that place, Savage didn't blame her.

The footage was black-and-white. Grainy. Low resolution, with a halo of smoke and dust hovering in the frame. Still, you could make out most of the faces.

"It'll do," Savage muttered.

Thorpe moved the timeline forward. "This is 20:00 hours, the night of the murder."

"There's Zeb." Savage pointed to the screen. As he'd stated, Zeb was sitting at a corner table with two guys, drinking beer out of a bottle and by the looks of things, talking shit. Savage could tell by their stance that they were shooting the breeze, not discussing anything heavy.

They drank, they laughed, then drank some more.

"Looks like he was telling the truth," Thorpe said, leaning back in his chair.

"Run it forward a couple of hours," Savage instructed.

They watched in silence as the timeline jumped ahead. Characters blinked in and out like ghosts. At 22:30 Zeb stood, shuffled to the bar, grabbed more beers, then hit the men's room. He was gone less than five minutes.

"He's in the clear," Savage said when the reel ticked past midnight and a very drunk Zeb stumbled out of the bar. "His alibi checks out."

"Can't believe he rode home in that state." Thorpe scowled at the screen. "It's a miracle he made it."

Savage frowned, deep in thought. Zeb couldn't have done it. Axle was already dead by midnight, his body gathering dust in the quarry. Besides, in that condition, Zeb was only heading to one place. Bed.

It was the movement on the way out that caught Savage's eye. "Hold up," he said, blinking at the screen.

"What?" Thorpe asked.

He gestured with his hand. "Play that back."

Thorpe rewound the footage.

"Okay. Now watch the door." Savage nodded to the visuals playing out in front of them.

Zeb stumbled out, ricocheting off the door frame as he went. He brushed past another biker, then disappeared into the dark parking lot.

"See that?" Savage pointed.

Thorpe shook his head. "What am I looking at?"

"Joel."

"The barman?"

"Yeah, Joel is coming in at four minutes past midnight. Zeb bumps into him on his way out."

108

DUST DEVIL

"Yeah, so?"

"So the time of Axle's death was between eight and midnight. Let's back up and see what time Joel left the bar."

Thorpe sucked in a breath, catching on. He reversed the feed again, slowly.

At 21:47, Joel slipped out into the night. He didn't reappear until he passed Zeb at the front door two hours later.

"He left just before ten and got back at midnight," Savage murmured. "That puts him outside the bar the entire window of Axle's estimated time of death."

Thorpe's face hardened. "You think he did it?"

Savage stared at the screen. "Could've, yeah."

"But why would Joel kill Axle?"

Savage tightened his jaw. "For Rosalie."

"You mean she organized it?"

Savage gave a grim nod. "I can't see him doing it without her say-so."

"He is the newbie," Sinclair said, coming over to join them at Thorpe's desk. "He'd be desperate to prove himself."

"Let's hope he's not willing to go to prison for her." Savage looked at his deputies. "Sinclair, take Lucas with you and bring him in. It's time we had a heart to heart with the Crimson Angels' newest member."

JOEL SAT STIFFLY in the interview chair, his hands flat on the metal table, his jaw locked tight. He looked more like a soldier waiting for deployment than a suspect in a murder case. He wore khaki cargo pants, heavy biker boots, and his black T-shirt hugged his muscular frame.

Savage shut the door and dropped into the chair across from him. Joel shifted but didn't speak.

"You know why you're here?" Savage asked. Sinclair would have already cautioned him and asked if he wanted a lawyer present.

109

Joel didn't answer.

Savage studied him. He didn't look like a killer, but then, he'd given up making assumptions about suspects a long time ago. The young biker's posture was rigid, he looked uptight, but not nervous. More like he resented being here. Not an uncommon reaction to being brought in for questioning.

Savage got straight to it. "We need to ask you some questions about the night Axle Weston was murdered. You've waived your right to a lawyer, yes?"

"Got nothing to hide."

Fair enough. "Where were you between ten and midnight on July 27th?"

"I was at the Roadhouse."

Why lie? "No, you weren't. You were seen leaving the bar around ten o'clock, and you didn't get back until just after midnight." He didn't mention the camera footage—Rosalie would kill him. Besides, without a warrant, it wouldn't be admissible in court anyway.

Joel gave him a hard look. "I went for a ride."

"For two hours?"

The biker shrugged. "It was a hot night. I needed some air."

Lately, every night was a hot night.

"Anyone with you?"

"Nope."

"You sure about that?"

"Yeah, I'm sure. I just said so, didn't I?"

Savage leaned forward. "Listen, kid. I've got a dead former president in a quarry, your boss's motorcycle at the crime scene, and you unaccounted for during the exact window of the murder."

Joel slid his hands off the table and put them in his lap.

Savage set a crime scene photo down in front of him. Axle's body, covered in dirt, a large red stain darkening his shirt.

Joel glanced at it but didn't flinch. "I didn't kill him."

Savage tilted his head. "Where'd you go then?"

"I don't know, man. Around."

Savage studied him, letting the silence draw out. Joel didn't fidget. Didn't glance at the camera or back down at the crime scene photo. He didn't do any of the things suspects usually did when he let the tension build like this.

"If there's anyone who can alibi you," Savage said, eventually. The kid was as calm as a cucumber, or he was innocent. "Now's the time to tell me, because this isn't looking good for you."

Still, Joel didn't answer.

Savage leaned back in his chair. "You're hiding something, Joel. Problem is, I don't know what. You know what that means?"

Joel shook his head.

"It means we're going to assume the worst and charge you with Axle Weston's murder."

Joel's eyes flicked up at that. "I swear, man. I didn't kill him. I didn't even know the guy."

That was true. Joel had joined the club after Rosalie had taken over as president.

Savage narrowed his gaze, frustrated. "Then why not tell me where you went?"

Joel just shook his head, tightlipped.

Savage drew in a slow breath, giving himself time to think. If Joel was innocent, why wouldn't he say where he was? Then it struck him. He was protecting someone.

And there was only one person he'd go out of his way like this to protect. Only one person whose wrath was worse than the Sheriff Department's.

Rosalie.

"Was Rosalie with you?" Savage asked quietly.

Joel's pupils dilated. It was a micro expression, but Savage caught it.

Bingo.

"Did you give her a ride out to the quarry so she could shoot her ex-husband? Is that where you went?"

Joel's jaw popped with tension. Savage was getting warm.

They'd been so intent on analyzing Zeb's movements, and then Joel's, that they hadn't thought to look for Rosalie in the footage.

"Once she'd shot him, you brought her back to the Roadhouse."

"No," he growled.

Savage fixed his gaze on Joel's face.

"You were with Rosalie that night, weren't you? That's why you disappeared. That's why you've got no alibi. Because you won't give her up."

He just shook his head, but he looked worried. Savage knew he was onto something, he just couldn't believe Rosalie had lied to him about this.

Why was he surprised?

He exhaled wearily. "Wait here."

Savage left the interview room, strode back to the bullpen, and up to Thorpe's desk. "Where was Rosalie Weston that night? Was she in the bar footage?"

"I'll check for you."

Thorpe got straight to work, his fingers flying over the keyboard.

Savage, too keyed up to sit down, paced the squadroom while he waited.

When would he learn not to trust anything Rosalie said?

Barb shot him a concerned look. "You want a coffee?"

"No, thanks." More caffeine might just send him over the edge.

"You were right," Thorpe said, ten minutes later.

Savage's heart sank.

Shit.

"Rosalie's not there. I've checked the whole lot, and she goes to her office around a quarter to eight and doesn't emerge until after twelve."

"She could have been working," Sinclair offered, coming over.

"There's a door leading from her office outside," Savage told them. "I've seen it."

"Like here?" Sinclair nodded in the direction of his office. He did the same thing, it helped avoid people he didn't want to see. Rosalie likely had it for the same reason.

"That means she could have gone with Joel to murder her ex-husband." Thorpe rubbed his forehead, perturbed.

Savage gave a slow nod. "That is what it's looking like."

"We can't prove it, though." Thorpe nodded at the footage. "This doesn't tell us where they went. It doesn't even prove they were together."

Savage grimaced. "That's the problem. I'll take another crack at Joel. He's determined not to give Rosalie up."

"It would mean the end of his club membership," Sinclair pointed out. "Could get messy for him if he ratted out the boss."

True. He remembered Rosalie's words.

Feuds happen. Sometimes people disappear. It's the way of the life.

Still, it was worth one more shot.

Savage returned to the interview room.

"Seems Rosalie Weston is unaccounted for that night too," he told Joel. "Kind of proves my theory, doesn't it?"

Joel eyed him warily. "It doesn't prove shit."

"Both of you missing on the same night? The night Axle Weston is gunned down at the quarry. Neither of you have an alibi, either. That stinks of conspiracy to me."

Joel shook his head. "You're wrong, man."

Savage's gaze hardened. "Am I? Why don't you tell me what happened then?"

Joel bit down on his lower lip.

Savage turned around. He was losing patience. "Fine, we'll see what Rosalie has to say."

Joel stiffened, and for a moment there Savage thought he'd break, but he kept his mouth shut.

Goddammit, the kid was tough. Or he'd been primed by Rosalie. Maybe threatened? Whatever the reason, he knew how to keep quiet.

Savage tried one more thing.

Taking out his cellphone, he dialed a number. "Yeah, it's me.

Arrest Rosalie Weston for the murder of her ex-husband, Axle Weston."

Joel's face twisted, but remarkably, he didn't utter a sound.

Savage could see his hands clench beneath the table. The guy was triggered, but he wasn't saying anything to incriminate himself or Rosalie.

Fair play to him.

Savage circled the table, Joel watching him warily. "I gave you a chance to come clean. Remember that."

When Joel didn't respond, Savage gave up and exited the room.

"Keep him here," he told Lucas, back in the bullpen. "Don't let him leave, but don't charge him yet either." Lucas nodded.

Savage turned to Thorpe. "I want his phone records, his GPS history, if we can pull it, and a warrant to search his place."

Thorpe got to work.

"You think he's protecting her?" Sinclair asked.

"I think they're protecting each other."

Savage strode back to his office and sat down. He'd just opened his laptop when he heard Barb say, "If you'll wait here, I'll see if the Sheriff is available."

"Let me in. Now," a sharp, female voice demanded.

His desk phone rang, but he knew what Barb would say before he answered. He picked up. "Yeah, you can let her in."

He heard Rosalie's heels as she stomped across the floor to his office. The door burst open and Rosalie stood there, all hellfire and brimstone, her dark hair flailing about her, green eyes flashing.

"Hello, Rosalie," he said.

She strode over to his desk and planted both hands down on it. "You arrested Joel?" There was disbelief in her voice. "I gave you that footage in good faith, and you arrested my bartender? What the hell, Dalton?"

The whole office was listening.

Calmly, Savage got up and closed the office door, giving them some privacy. "He's not under arrest."

She spun to face him. "Like hell he's not. You've got him in your interrogation room, haven't you?"

"I'm questioning him. He's a suspect in a homicide investigation."

"Joel didn't kill Axle."

Savage shrugged, refusing to argue. He'd never seen Rosalie so rattled, and for a lower-ranked prospect too. That was interesting.

"Well, he wasn't in the bar the night Axle was murdered. In fact, according to your video footage, he left around ten o'clock and only got back after midnight. That's two hours unaccounted for." He arched his eyebrows. "Just happens to be the two hours in which Axle was gunned down. How'd you explain that?"

She stared daggers at him.

He rested his hands on his hips. "Which brings me to another point. You weren't there either, Rosalie. Care to amend your story?"

If looks could kill, he'd be writhing in agony right now. "I have nothing to say to you. If you're not charging my guy, then I'm walking out of here with him right now."

Rosalie knew her rights.

They faced off, cold steel meeting fiery passion. "I can't let you do that. Joel has no alibi. I'm entitled to hold him for twenty-four hours while we pull his phone records, bank statements... basically upend his life."

She stiffened.

"What are we going to find, Rosalie?" Savage leaned back and studied her. She was hiding something, that was for sure, but he just wasn't sure it was murder. A flicker of an idea sparked in his brain.

She shook her head. "You're a pain in my goddamn ass, Dalton. You know that?"

He almost grinned.

"You were together, weren't you? He took you out to the quarry where you shot your ex-husband, then he transported you back to the Roadhouse."

He was baiting her, waiting for her to snap.

"That's not what happened," she hissed.

"Then tell me," he said softly.

She glared at him. With her flushed cheeks, gleaming eyes and flaring nostrils, she reminded him of a caged panther with nowhere left to turn.

"Oh, for fuck's sake. Yes, I was with him." She threw up her hands. "You happy now? But we didn't go out to the quarry. We went back to my place."

Savage gave a knowing nod. "You're in a relationship."

"No. Argh, yes." She glared at him. "We're just screwing, okay? It's not a relationship."

If that's all it was, why was she telling him? Why not leave Joel to sweat it out? She knew as well as he did that they couldn't prove anything. The footage would never stand up in court, yet Rosalie spared him the effort of grilling the kid. She was also risking her reputation if word of their affair ever got out. High stakes for the club president.

She had feelings for the new recruit. Maybe it wasn't love, but she felt more than she was letting on. It was refreshing, in a way. It proved she was human. That she had emotions, just like the rest of them.

Savage met her eyes. "Can you prove that?"

"That's what the bloody phone records are for," she huffed. "I'm sure you can ping our locations too." Then she turned and stormed out, the door slamming hard enough to rattle the blinds.

Savage stared at the closed door. Well, what do you know? If the phone records checked out, Rosalie and Joel were in the clear.

And they were no closer to finding Axle's killer.

NINETEEN

"JOEL AND ROSALIE?" Sinclair gawked at him. "I don't believe it."

Savage gave an amused nod. "It's true, I saw it in her eyes. There's definitely something going on there."

"But he's at least ten years younger than her, plus he's a prospect. She's the freaking club president."

"Guess that means she can do whatever the hell she likes." Lucas grinned at Sinclair.

"I'm not saying she can't, I just mean it's so unlike her to—"

"Stoop so low?" Thorpe interjected.

Sinclair threw up her hands. "Yeah, hierarchically speaking. I'm just surprised, that's all. Anyway, it doesn't matter. If they were together, then they didn't shoot Axle."

"I'm checking CCTV in the vicinity of Rosalie's house now," Thorpe said. "There's no eyes on her street, but there's a traffic camera a couple of roads before, and they'd have to go that way to get to hers."

"Keep me posted." Savage turned and headed for the door. "I'm going to grab something to eat. Anyone want anything?"

They all shook their heads. It was mid-afternoon and they'd

probably already eaten. Instead of getting his sub order to go like he normally did, he decided to sit down for a while, let his thoughts settle.

Rosalie's confession had side-swiped him too, changing the direction of the investigation. Again. First it was Axle, then Zeb, then Rosalie and Joel, and now...

Now what?

Diesel's remains had opened up a festering wound within the Crimson Angels, that much was clear. Tensions were high, and now Axle had been murdered too. Related, yes. Same shooter? Probably not. The style of their second victim was different from the first. Haphazard, two misses, one hit—when he was already on the ground.

Savage went back to the beginning and thought through what he knew. Diesel had been distributing drugs for Zeb, who'd gotten them from a corrupt colleague on the force back in Denver. That much was confirmed.

Typical Zeb, but he'd gone behind Axle's back and recruited Diesel to sell them for him. They'd both made some extra cash on the side, without anyone knowing.

Or did someone find out?

Had Axle known? Had he discovered what they were doing and killed Diesel for cutting him out? You didn't do that in the MC. Loyalty was everything, and betrayal almost certainly meant death.

He chewed thoughtfully. Rosalie claimed not to have any knowledge of Diesel's betrayal and not much passed her by.

Next, there was Zeb himself. It was feasible he'd gotten rid of his partner-in-crime to prevent Diesel ratting him out. If under pressure from Axle, Diesel might have confessed everything in the hopes he'd be spared.

Except Zeb had been in the bar all night. That was also indisputable.

He frowned, as he considered the various angles. Diesel had wanted out. He'd wanted to make a life with Honey Granger and their unborn child, so he might have taken the side hustle with Zeb to fund that. In that case, it's unlikely he'd have told Axle what they were doing. There's no way he'd have put Honey and his child in the firing line. If you took that into account, Zeb had no reason to silence him.

Diesel's brawl with the logger, Nathan Wood, had come to nothing. A possessive boyfriend flexing his muscles, that was all. It showed he'd really cared about Honey. That was reassuring.

Then there was Scooter and his statement. A possible shady deal between Axle Weston and Sheriff Jeffries. Was that relevant, or just normal club business? Greasing palms to look the other way. Not uncommon, unfortunately. Jeffries was corrupt, sure, but was he a murderer? Knowing the man, Savage didn't think so.

Savage finished his lunch and stretched, ironing out the kinks in his back. So many ifs and buts. Nothing definitive.

One question kept plaguing him.

Why had Axle escaped now? Was it really just a matter of seizing the moment? Prison transfers were the weak link in the system. Everybody knew that. There were fewer guards. No reinforced cells. No barbed wire. Just a van, a schedule, and a window of vulnerability.

He scratched his head. Somehow, the timing felt deliberate. Was it because Rosalie was solidifying her position as president, and Axle wanted to unseat her before his influence slipped away completely? Being behind bars had weakened his hold. Under Rosalie's leadership, the club was stronger than ever—and Axle was losing face. Not that he could've reclaimed his position, not with a life sentence looming. Still, parole was always a possibility.

Maybe it was just plain old revenge that drove his escape. Rosalie had put him behind bars—so now, she had to pay.

Only someone had taken him out of the equation first. But who? He stared into his empty coffee cup.

Back to square one.

"Sheriff, fancy seeing you here."

The voice made him flinch. He glanced up. "Councilman Beckett."

They shook hands.

"Mind if I join you?"

The last thing he wanted, but he gestured to the vacant seat opposite. "Sure."

Beckett eased his suited frame into it. "How are things? I heard you got the fugitive, Axle Weston."

"Well, we found his body, if that's what you mean."

"Good work," he said, as if Savage had personally been responsible. "Any idea who shot him?"

"Nope." Even if he did, he wouldn't share the details with the councilman. "We're following multiple leads."

"I can't say I'm surprised," he said with a nod. "That biker gang is nothing but trouble."

"They haven't been for a while," Savage corrected, not entirely sure why he was defending them. Rosalie kept the club's illicit activities under wraps, and a tight rein on her members. There hadn't been any brawling, unwanted trouble or unnecessary disruptions for some time now. Nothing that had warranted law enforcement's intervention, anyway.

Beckett wasn't convinced. "Axle Weston was a bad apple. The world is a safer place without him."

Savage didn't disagree.

"How are those proposals coming on?" he asked, knowing Barb would want him to chase it up.

"Good. Good," Beckett replied. "I put in a word and the committee has approved your requests."

"That's great." Savage managed a genuine grin. Some good news at last. The whole department would be elated.

"Happy to be of service," Beckett said, getting to his feet. "It was good talking with you, Sheriff." He leaned forward, over the table. "Just between us, I know there are a lot of people who want to see the back of that outlaw motorcycle club. Make that happen, and you'll have a lot of support behind you. This is only the beginning of what we can achieve together."

He gave a friendly nod before striding out of the coffee shop in his cowboy boots. Savage scowled after him.

That sounded like a bribe if he'd ever heard one.

SAVAGE GOT BACK to the office to find the place in an uproar. Honey Granger's mother stood in the center of the squad room, tears streaming down her face.

"What's going on?" he murmured to Barb on the way in.

"Honey's missing," she whispered back.

"Really? Shit."

He strode up to the distraught woman and put a hand on her shoulder. "Mrs. Granger, do you want to come into my office? You can tell me what happened."

"I'm so worried," she said, sniffing as she followed him in. "It's not like her to just vanish."

Savage gestured to a chair. "Please, take a seat. Barb, can you fetch Mrs. Granger a glass of water?"

Barb nodded and hurried to the kitchen.

"Okay, now why don't you start at the beginning. When did you first notice Honey was missing?"

"She left with Ben this morning, as usual, but didn't take him to school. Then the diner called and said she hadn't arrived at work. At first I thought she must have gotten a flat or something, but when she didn't answer her phone, I began to worry."

"Both Honey and her son are missing?" he asked.

"Yeah, that's why I'm so worried. She'd never take him out of school. Not even for a day."

Savage frowned. "And she didn't have an appointment or anything else today that she didn't tell you about?"

"No, I would have known."

A heavy feeling settled in his stomach. This was not good. "Did you report this to Sheriff Shelby?"

The Durango sheriff was her first point of call. After all, they went missing in his jurisdiction.

"I did, yes. But he said I couldn't report them missing yet. I had to wait twenty-four hours." She blinked away more tears, and he nodded.

"That is usually the case, yes."

Shelby wouldn't have known Honey's history. Wouldn't have known that she and her son's disappearance may be linked to another investigation.

"That's why I came here. Will you find them? I'm so worried something terrible has happened."

"We will put out a BOLO on them, yes," Savage decided. He had to admit, not taking her son to school or going to work were both bright red flags.

"We'll also ping her cellphone, try to find out where she is."

Mrs. Granger leaned over and clutched his hand. "Thank you, Sheriff. I knew you'd help me."

He only hoped he could.

TWENTY

"HER PHONE'S OFF," said Thorpe, once Barb had escorted the distressed Mrs. Granger out. He'd sprung into action as soon as he'd heard what had happened. Savage stood behind him, hands on hips, watching the screen.

"Last known location?"

Thorpe clicked through the ping data. "Her son's school. 07:54 AM."

Sinclair got up and came over. "I thought her mother said she didn't take him to school."

"She didn't take him inside," corrected Thorpe. "Whatever happened... happened there."

"We need to get out there," Savage said.

"I'll call Sheriff Shelby." Sinclair reached for her cell. "Let him know you're coming."

Savage turned to his newest deputy. "Lucas, you're riding with me."

. . .

L.T. RYAN

THEY ARRIVED at the daycare mid-morning. The parking lot was quiet, the midday lull settling in. Savage showed his badge at the front desk, and within minutes, they were led to the vice principal's office.

Mrs. Kramer was mid-to-late forties, wearing a wrinkled blazer, worry lines etched into her forehead. She stood as they entered.

"You're here about Honey Granger?" She wrung her hands in front of her like a dishcloth.

"That's right," Savage said. "We understand she arrived at daycare this morning but didn't bring Ben inside?"

A quick nod. "It was the strangest thing. One of our teachers saw Honey in the parking lot, but Ben never came to class. We're not sure why."

"Someone saw her?" Lucas clarified.

"Yes, Mrs. Glick saw Honey's car pull into the lot before daycare. Apparently she didn't park, just looped around and drove back out onto the street."

"We'll need to speak to Mrs. Glick," Savage said. "But first, do you have any surveillance cameras situated around the school?"

"We do," the vice principal replied. "But not in the parking lot. Only the front and back entrances, and the playground."

Damn. He controlled his disappointment. It was never going to be that easy.

"Come with me," she said, brushing past them. "Mrs. Glick will just be finishing her lesson."

They followed her down a brightly lit corridor decorated with student artwork. Savage admired the stick figures, construction paper trees, and glitter-covered posters about recycling and kindness.

It looked like a great place. Warm, with good values. He hoped his own son would attend somewhere like this one day.

A pang sliced through him. Ben wasn't much older than Connor and he was missing, along with his mother. Both out there somewhere, vulnerable and alone.

124

DUST DEVIL

They reached the end of the hall. Sunlight streamed through a pair of wide glass doors, and beyond them, Savage could hear the echo of children's laughter on the playground.

He had to find them.

Turning left, they entered a classroom that looked like it belonged in an advertising brochure. The walls were painted a soft pastel yellow and covered in motivational posters. A dreamcatcher made of bottle tops and ribbons hung near the open window, rattling in the breeze.

There was a cozy reading nook in the corner, and in the front of the class, a guinea pig snoozed in a cage labeled: Captain Nibbles.

Mrs. Glick stood beside her desk. She had dark hair braided down her back and wore an embroidered Mexican-style jacket over a flowing skirt. She gave off a serene energy, despite the current crisis.

The vice principal leaned in and whispered something. Mrs. Glick nodded and gently clapped her hands twice. "Alright, explorers," she said. "Time to head out for recess. You know the drill. Quiet feet, kind words."

The toddlers filed out with the practiced chaos of preschoolers. A few offered waves to Savage and Lucas on their way past.

Once the last child had gone, Mrs. Glick turned her warm, intelligent gaze toward them. "You're here about Honey, right?"

Savage nodded. "We understand you may have seen her vehicle this morning."

Mrs. Glick tucked a loose strand of hair behind her ear and motioned for them to sit. "I did, yes. Honey usually drops Ben off at eight o'clock, sometimes a little before. He's a sweet kid—quiet, polite. Adores Captain Nibbles."

Lucas opened his mouth, then his gaze turned to the hamster cage, and he nodded.

"What about this morning?"

"This morning was... strange." She lowered her voice. "I was walking back from the playground with another teacher. We'd just

125

finished morning yard duty. I saw Honey's car drive into the lot, but she didn't get out."

Savage narrowed his gaze. "Did you see her?"

Mrs. Glick nodded. "Yes. She was in the driver's seat. Ben was in the back. I didn't see him clearly, but I definitely recognized her profile. She looked... tense. Hands gripping the wheel. She just sat there. I thought maybe she was taking a call."

"Anyone else in the car?"

"I don't think so. After a few minutes, she drove off. Didn't let Ben out—just pulled away suddenly and took off out of the lot."

He frowned. "What time was this?"

"About 7:55. Just before the bell."

Savage frowned. "You're certain it was her?"

"Positive. I know her well."

"Would you say she looked spooked?"

"The way she took off out of there, yeah, I'd say something freaked her out. No idea what, though."

"So, she didn't usually stick around and chat with other parents?"

Mrs. Glick shook her head. "No, Honey was always in a hurry. She has a job to get to, at Lou's Diner."

Savage nodded and stood. "I know it. Thank you, Mrs. Glick. That helps."

"I hope she's all right," the teacher said, genuine worry in her voice.

He did too.

OUTSIDE, Savage and Lucas got into the Suburban. Savage scanned the daycare parking lot, picturing Honey driving in, stopping, then looping around and taking off again.

"Maybe she saw something or someone," Lucas suggested, "and it frightened her."

"She'd have to be pretty spooked to take off like that," he agreed.

"Damn shame about the cameras," Lucas said. "They could do with some out here."

"Let's swing by Lou's Diner." Savage started the engine. "See if her boss knows anything about why she disappeared."

FIFTEEN MINUTES LATER, they pushed open the door to the diner. Lucas looked around and then aimed for the rotund guy in the red apron.

"Remember me?" he said, coming to a stop beside him.

The man nodded. "Of course, Deputy. What can I do for you?"

"This is Sheriff Savage from Hawk's Landing. We need to speak to you privately about Honey Granger."

He wiped his hands on his apron, then nodded and gestured for them to follow him. They walked to the back of the diner, where a four-seater table stood open. "Take a seat."

"Is Honey okay? Her mom already called here."

"She's disappeared," Savage said briskly. "We're trying to piece together her last known whereabouts. Did you hear from her this morning?"

Tony shook his head. "No, not a thing. I figured maybe her kid was sick or something, you know?"

Savage nodded.

"Anything out of the ordinary happen yesterday?" he asked.

Tony hesitated. "Well, she was upset after you'd spoken to her. I understand she got some bad news?"

Savage gave a tight nod.

"I told her to take some time. I was worried about her, but she insisted ten minutes was enough. She went out back."

"Okay, why's that strange?" asked Savage.

The manager's gaze drifted to the window. "Because, when I went outside for a smoke, I heard her talking on the phone."

Where was this going? "Yeah?"

"She had two phones. One at her ear, and the other in her hand. I've only ever seen her with the one."

Savage frowned. "Are you sure?"

"Positive. She's worked here for over three years, and I've never seen her with a second phone."

Savage and Lucas exchanged a glance.

"Could you tell who she was talking to?" asked Savage.

"No. She was too far away."

"Did she leave early?" Lucas asked.

"No, Honey wasn't like that. She worked her shift, but she was definitely quieter than usual, like her head was someplace else."

Savage tapped his fingers on the counter. A secret phone. And now she was gone. So was her son.

"You got security footage?" he asked.

Tony gestured to the camera above the register. "Covers the register and front door only. Nothing out back."

Savage gave a tight nod. Times were tough. People weren't splurging on surveillance. "Okay, thanks for talking with us. If Honey contacts you, call me directly." He passed over a card.

"Sure thing, Sheriff."

Back in the truck, Lucas glanced over. "Two phones. That's never a good sign."

"No," Savage agreed. "It's not."

He stared through the windshield, brain ticking over. "The question is: who was on the other end of that call?"

And were they the reason Honey and Ben had vanished?

TWENTY-ONE

"THERE'S no record of Honey Granger owning a second phone," Thorpe told them later at the Sheriff's Office. The sun had set by the time they got back to Hawk's Landing, but as usual, the whole team was still there.

"It must be prepaid," Savage said, his jaw set. "A burner."

"Never registered," Thorpe agreed. "She kept it completely off the grid."

"Check her bank activity anyway. See if there's anything unusual —cash withdrawals, trips out of county. Anything suspicious."

"On it."

Barb rushed into the squad room. "It's Mason on Line 2, for Sinclair. Doesn't sound good."

Sinclair shot him a worried look and picked up her desk phone. After a few clipped words, her expression changed.

"Okay, we'll be right there." She lowered the handset, already moving for her gear.

"What's happened?" asked Lucas.

"The wind's shifted," she told them. "There are flare-ups along the east ridge now. Mason's calling in all hands. They're evacuating Maple Hollow and Hillcrest."

"Shit." Savage strode back to his office to grab his fire kit and keys. This was the worst possible time.

Making a snap decision, he said, "Lucas, with me. Sinclair, take the cruiser and notify Shelby on the way. We'll need backup units from Durango to help with traffic and evac."

Sinclair nodded, already halfway to the door.

"What about Honey?" Thorpe asked, swinging round in his chair.

Savage paused. "Keep combing her financials, see what you can find. Notify local units, put out a missing persons alert on her and her son. If anything changes, call me directly. Right now, we've got lives to save."

"HOLY SHIT," Savage muttered.

The fire was everywhere. A hot, whirling gale had whipped sparks over the containment lines, setting off a multitude of brush-fires. By the time they arrived at the staging zone, the entire side of the mountain had become a furnace.

Flames engulfed the trees and shrubs, while smoke unfurled above them like a tidal wave. In the distance, they could hear sirens wailing as the emergency support vehicles tore through the valley.

Mason met them, his face streaked with soot, his helmet tucked under one arm. Sinclair stood beside him, pale with worry. "We've got flare-ups near Maple Street with embers jumping two hundred feet. We've got to push the line north, or we lose the Hollow."

Savage nodded. "What do you need?"

"Mass evacuations. We need to set up traffic blocks and keep people out of the canyon."

"Done." He turned to Lucas, who was already on the phone, as well as gesturing to locals and onlookers to get back. "Coordinate the roadblock with Shelby."

Lucas nodded and strode off, phone still glued to his ear.

DUST DEVIL

"I'll start banging on doors." Sinclair headed in the direction of the shower of ash.

"Be careful," Mason called after her. "This thing's erratic as hell."

She turned and gave him a thumbs up.

Savage made himself useful and manned a choke point with Mason's men, waving evacuees through and rerouting sightseers who hadn't gotten the memo to stay out. Every hour, the situation worsened.

Dry pine needles ignited instantly. The gusts blew sideways, carrying embers over firebreaks and into backyards. A propane tank went up near the pass with a bang that rattled windows three blocks over.

By midnight, Savage was bone-tired. His shirt clung to his back. His eyes burned from the smoke, but he hadn't heard anything from Thorpe, so he pressed on.

It was nearly 1:00 a.m. when a fresh team from Pagosa Springs rocked up. Mason told Savage and his team to back down. "Thanks for your help. PSFD will take over."

"You get some rest too," Savage told him, thumping him on the back. The fire chief looked ready to drop.

Savage had just collapsed into his SUV when the police radio crackled.

"Sheriff, it's Firefighter Jill Sloane from Station Three. We found something that might interest you."

Savage keyed his mic. "Go ahead."

"We've got a vehicle fire at the north end of Hillcrest Drive. The flames are out but it's still smoldering. From what we can tell, the make and model match the BOLO on that Honda Civic registered to one Honey Granger."

A pause crackled across the line.

Savage felt his weary pulse accelerate. "Any sign of the occupants?"

"Can't say yet. It's too burned out to tell. We'll have to wait until it cools down to do a proper inspection. You might want to send CSU out to take a look."

His stomach sank.

God no.

Please don't let her and her kid be in there.

"On my way."

TWENTY-TWO

THE VEHICLE WAS A WRECK. Melted, collapsed and warped from heat. Flames still licked the interior, and the entire structure was smoking worse than a barbeque.

"It's too hot to touch," a firefighter told him. "Going to be a couple of hours before we can get near it."

"I'll wait." He wasn't going anywhere until he knew for sure that Honey Granger and her son were not in that car.

Savage leaned on the hood of the Suburban, arms crossed, watching as Pearl stepped out of her Tahoe. She looked as wrecked as he felt, her eyes red-rimmed from smoke, her short, gray hair damp with sweat, but her movements steady.

"You been up all night?" he asked her.

The wildfires had finally begun to subside. The wind had dropped sometime around dawn, and left behind scorched ground, hollowed homes and a plume of lingering smoke that hung above the valley like a bruise.

She nodded, pulling on a pair of gloves. "Ray and I have been at the community center treating residents for smoke inhalation, among other things. Looks like you have too?"

He shrugged. "Got a missing mother and kid."

She scanned the blackened shell of a vehicle. "This her car?"

"Yeah. Matches the plate." He straightened, shoulders stiff from too many hours in a fire vest. "We haven't touched the inside."

Pearl pulled on shoe coverings, then crouched beside the driver's door, which had melted to its hinges. She pulled out a flashlight and peered into the black cavity behind that once held seats, carpet, and a family.

Her eyes narrowed in the dim beam. "It's bad. But not hot enough to destroy bone."

"You sure?"

Pearl didn't answer right away. She moved down the vehicle and opened the backseat door, shining her light inside. The air still reeked of scorched plastic and fuel. The booster seat was warped beyond recognition, a fossil of a thing.

"No skeletal remains," she confirmed. "Not even fragments."

"What about the trunk?"

A fire officer had prized it open earlier, but he hadn't wanted to touch it until she'd gotten there.

Gingerly, she lifted the hood. There was nothing inside, other than burned carpeting and the acrid smell of burned rubber from the spare. Savage let out a ragged breath he hadn't realized he'd been holding.

Pearl straightened up and pulled off her gloves with a snap. "If they were in this vehicle when it burned, we'd know." She looked across at him. "That doesn't help much, though, does it?"

He shook his head. "No. They're still missing."

Pearl gave him a sympathetic look. "Go home, Dalton. Get some sleep. You're no good to anyone like this."

"I will, as soon as I find them."

She sighed, patted his shoulder, and walked back to her car. "I'll take some samples, then get a report started. If anything changes once we get the results back, I'll let you know. For now—no bodies, no blood, no biological traces I can see."

"Appreciate it." He watched her kit up in her full forensic suit to process the wreck. If they weren't in that car, then where the hell were they?

THE SMOKEY HAZE was lifting and the sun was beating down when he finally drove back to the office. The team were in, albeit bleary-eyed. He hoped they'd managed to get some sleep.

Sinclair sat at her desk, coffee cup in hand, reviewing traffic cam footage from the day before. Thorpe was on the phone with Durango PD, probably checking area surveillance or hospital admissions. Lucas was running DMV searches on known associates of Zeb and Axle.

"Anything?" he asked, hopefully.

Thorpe shook his head. "Still no pings on Honey's phone. I widened the radius to include every burner registered in a thirty-mile radius this month. Nothing popped. Either she's off-grid—or someone made sure she is."

Savage nodded, ran a hand through his hair. "What about the BOLO?"

"Nothing apart from her vehicle last night."

Knowing he must smell pretty bad, Savage disappeared into the locker room, stripped off his smoke-stained clothes, and stood under the freezing water until his skin prickled.

There were no clean towels, just paper towels from the dispenser, but he didn't care. It felt good to be clean.

He changed into the spare clothes he kept in his locker. Jeans, a fresh T-shirt, and a department-issued button-down. No time to shave, although maybe he should have. His reflection in the mirror shocked him. Hollow-eyed and strung out, he'd never looked or felt worse.

When he stepped back into the bullpen, Sinclair handed him a coffee without saying a word. They worked in silence for another

L.T. RYAN

hour, following threads that went nowhere. No ransom note. No bodies. No sightings. Nothing.

Where the hell was she?

At 11:12, his phone rang.

He recognized the number and stiffened.

Zeb.

He answered with a bark. "Unless you're calling to confess, I don't have time for this."

The former cop exhaled into the phone. "Dalton, you need to get out here."

Savage could hear it in his voice something was terribly wrong. "Why? What's happened?"

There was a pause on the line. Too long. Then a muffled sound in the background like someone crying.

Savage's gut tightened. "Zeb—what the hell's going on?"

"One of my Johns died last night. Tonya found him. She's a goddamn mess."

Savage could still hear the uncontrolled sobbing in the background, louder now.

"Who is it?"

"Walter Minstrel."

Shit.

Savage rubbed a hand over his jaw. "Okay. I'm on my way. Don't touch anything."

"Yeah, yeah. I know the drill."

He hung up.

Savage stared at the phone for a long beat, then got up and walked into the bullpen. "Lucas, with me. We're heading to the Hidden Gem," he said grimly. "Zeb says Walter Minstrel's dead."

"Another biker?"

Savage gave a grim nod.

Sinclair looked up. "You don't want me to come with you?"

"No, you keep abreast of the fire situation. Call me if anything changes. Thorpe, keep going on Honey Granger."

DUST DEVIL

Thorpe gave a concise nod and turned back to his screen.

Sinclair sighed. "There are bikers turning up dead all over the place. What the hell is going on?"

"No idea. But whatever it is... I get the feeling Honey Granger is right in the middle of it."

TWENTY-THREE

SAVAGE, accompanied by Lucas, pulled into the Hidden Gem Trailer Park just after ten in the morning. The sun was already climbing, burning through the early haze, casting long slats of light between the trees. He hadn't slept more than an hour, and his head ached from exhaustion and tension.

Zeb waited out front, pacing the dirt track with a cigarette pinched tight between his fingers. His sweaty T-shirt clung to his thin frame. He looked rattled. For once there was no smirk, no swagger—just drawn and quiet.

Savage got out of the Suburban. Lucas followed behind, lugging the field kit.

Savage didn't bother with preamble. "What happened?"

Zeb glanced over his shoulder, then sighed. "An hour ago, Tonya ran into the house screaming. When I could get some sense out of her, I went to take a look in the trailer and—" He shook his head. "Well, you can see for yourself."

He motioned for them to follow.

They cut behind Zeb's sprawling mobile home and around to three rusty old trailers, some sagging with age, others propped up with cinder blocks. The grass around them was overgrown and filled with weeds. It was obvious the trailers had been stationary for a long time. This was the informal "brothel" Zeb's girls worked out of.

Zeb gestured to a faded white-and-blue trailer. A busted screen door creaked in the breeze. Outside, Tonya sat on an upturned crate, her mascara smeared halfway down her cheeks. Her whole body trembled as she rocked back and forth in a futile attempt to comfort herself.

She wore a thin tank top that looked like it had been spray-painted red it had so much blood on it, the strap falling off one shoulder. Her hair was messed up, and there were red smears all down the left side of her body.

"She's not making much sense," Zeb said.

Lucas stopped beside the sex worker. "I'll try to calm her down, see what I can get out of her."

"Oh God, oh God." Tonya sobbed harder when she realized the sheriff and his deputies had arrived. Her eyes were wide, pupils still dilated. "I didn't do this—I swear to God—I didn't—I woke up and—"

"I know," Savage heard Lucas murmur. "Let's get you inside and sit you down, all right? You can tell me everything."

"Don't let her change her clothes," Savage called after him. "Pearl will want to see her just like that."

Lucas nodded before leading her away from the horrors inside the trailer.

Savage stepped up to the door and peered inside.

"Jeez" he hissed, freezing at the sight that greeted him. Walter Minstrel lay on his back on the bed, shirtless, one arm flung over his stomach, the other dangling limply off the mattress. His throat had been sliced deep and wide—nearly ear to ear.

Most shocking were the walls covered in blood spatter. It reminded Savage of a Jackson Pollock exhibition he'd seen once with Becca. Beneath the body, the sheets were black with dried blood.

Even more disturbing, the victim's eyes were open as if he'd been staring up at his attacker.

Savage let out a long breath as he stepped back down onto the grass. He'd seen enough to know this was a vicious, premedicated attack. That kind of carnage was not incidental. "We need forensics out here."

Behind him, Zeb groaned.

"Looks like he bled out on the bed," he told Zeb. "Blood spatter everywhere."

"I noticed."

At Savage's sharp look, he added, "Don't worry, I didn't go inside. Stopped at the doorway once I saw the state of him, just like you." Zeb shifted, unsettled. Savage didn't blame him. It took a lot to shake the former Denver detective, but even he had a limit.

Savage turned and examined the trailer's doorframe.

Zeb shook his head. "No sign of forced entry that I could see, but the trailer would have been unlocked, since—" He petered off. "Well, you know. It was occupied."

"Yeah." Savage straightened up. Maybe the sex worker had seen something. Then again, judging by the wild-eyed state of her, maybe not. That was probably the only reason she was still alive.

Savage's suspicions were confirmed when Lucas emerged from Zeb's house, shaking his head. "She claims she passed out cold. They did a little oxy before they got down to business, and afterwards, she blacked out. Walter was alive and well at that stage. When she woke up, she found him like that." He nodded to the trailer.

"You believe her?" asked Savage.

He gave a nod. "Poor thing's traumatized. She's covered in his blood and can't wash it off."

"Not till she's been swabbed," Savage insisted.

Lucas grimaced. "I've suggested counseling."

Savage knew she wouldn't take him up on it. It would mean admitting what she did for a living, and getting help for her drug addiction, neither of which earned her any money. She'd be back at work, higher than ever, before too long. It was a vicious cycle, doing drugs to take the edge off what they did, then getting paid, and blowing it all on drugs the next night. Very few got out of the game. Honey Granger was one of the lucky ones.

"Did you manage to establish a timeline?" Savage asked.

"She claims Walter arrived just after eleven, and she fell asleep around one, although she can't be sure."

"I heard the Harley pull around back around eleven," Zeb confirmed.

Savage glanced behind the trailer. "His motorcycle still there?"

Zeb nodded. "Yeah."

Savage's phone beeped.

He glanced down. "Ray and Pearl are on their way."

The pair had been kept busy this week. So much for a quiet retirement.

"COME TO HAWK'S LANDING, they said. Nothing ever happens there," were the first words out of Pearl's mouth when she and her husband arrived at the crime scene.

Savage snorted. "Sorry about this. I can call a team from Durango, if you'd prefer."

"We're here now," Ray grumbled, already unzipping his kit.

Secretly, Savage thought the pair would be bored stiff if they had nothing to do. Both thrived on the chaos of a crime scene, making sense of the mystery surrounding the deaths.

Savage explained what had happened, then left them to kit up and get on with it, not wanting to crowd the small space or compromise the crime scene.

They were inside for nearly an hour. When Ray came back out, his gloves were streaked with drying blood.

"Cause of death is clearly a severed throat. Transected the carotid and jugular. He would have been dead in minutes. Arterial blood spatter was immense, that's why the room and bed is covered in it."

"You should see the girl." Savage gestured to the house. "She's inside."

"I'll speak to her now," Pearl said, following her husband out. She carried her forensic kit case, battered from a lifetime of use.

"We'll need a tox report," Savage called after her.

Zeb appeared in the doorway. "I'll show you where she is."

Pearl disappeared inside with Zeb, while Savage turned back to Ray. "Find anything that will give us an idea who did this?"

"The killer used a fixed-blade knife. Probably a hunting blade," he said, narrowing his gaze. "I'll know more once I get him back to the lab, but it's the right length and depth. Also, your killer was left-handed."

Savage arched his brow. "That narrows it down. Are you sure?"

"Or ambidextrous. Your vic's throat was cut from right to left, signifying a left-handed blade holder. The length and force are consistent with someone using their dominant hand."

"Okay, great." That was something to go on at least.

"No murder weapon in sight," he added with a shrug. "The killer must have taken it with them."

"Has Pearl finished processing the scene?"

"Nope. She wants to bag the bedding once the body's been removed. Although to save time, we could simply take the whole trailer away," Ray said grimly, looking back at it.

"Fine with me," Zeb muttered.

Savage got it. Having police milling around was bad for business. Zeb just wanted them off his property, and out of the trailer park, as fast as possible.

"I'll arrange the tow," Lucas said, taking out his phone.

While he made the necessary arrangements, Pearl came out with Tonya's clothes in a clear evidence bag.

"She's a mess, but she'll live," she told them. "Once she cleans up and sobers up, she'll feel better."

Savage hoped so. "She mention anything of value?" Sometimes witnesses remembered more once the initial shock had worn off.

DUST DEVIL

Also, Tonya might open up more to a woman, especially one who wasn't a cop.

"Nope, but I took blood samples. We'll know if she's telling the truth about the oxy. Can't imagine she's lying, though, looking at the state of her."

Lucas had come to the same conclusion. Tonya was just an innocent bystander in all this. "She's lucky to be alive." Savage turned to Ray. "So how'd they do it then, if Walter was asleep when they came in?"

"Surprised him, is my guess." Ray pursed his lips thoughtfully. "I imagine Walter sat up, but by then, the killer was already beside the bed. Got him in a headlock and slit his throat before he had time to react."

"He would have been slow due to the drugs in his system," Savage mused. "Explains why he didn't put up a fight."

Ray nodded. "Probably a blessing. He wouldn't have known what was going on."

Savage grunted. It was a small comfort.

"Any chance this was a woman?"

Ray crinkled his forehead. "Judging by the strength needed to create that gash, I'd say not."

Savage knew there was a 'but' coming.

"But... as my wife is constantly reminding me, anything's possible. I wouldn't want to assume."

SAVAGE LEFT Lucas to make the necessary arrangements, then took Zeb aside. "You didn't hear anything during the night?"

"Nothing unusual. I mean, we're open for business till late, but after that it's usually pretty quiet."

"And you were here the whole time?"

"Yeah." He sighed. "Doesn't look good, does it?"

"Not in light of everything else that's been going on."

"This is connected, isn't it?" Zeb asked, rubbing his jaw. Once a cop, always a cop.

"Can't say for sure, but..." He shrugged. First Axle, then Walter. Someone was cleaning house. He wondered if Rosalie had anything to do with this.

"It wasn't her," Zeb said, as if reading his mind.

"Who?"

"You know who. Rosalie."

His gaze slanted. "What makes you say that?"

"It's not her style. I'm not saying she's not capable, but she wouldn't use violence unless it was absolutely necessary. Draws too much unwanted attention on the club, especially now, with the Diesel and Axle shit going down."

Savage looked toward the distant mountains, smoke still rising from the blackened ridges. He tended to agree.

"Besides, Walter came back into the fold. She gave him an ultimatum. The club or the highway, and he chose the club. There was no reason to bump him off."

Everything Zeb said made sense, but it didn't change the fact that Axle had been out to get revenge on Rosalie, to challenge her leadership, and threaten her life—and Walter had been his right-hand man. Now they were both dead.

"It still sends a message," Savage said grimly.

Zeb smoothed a hand over his spiky, balding head. "I know, but I just don't think this was her."

"Fair enough." He'd question her anyway. He wasn't about to take Zeb's word for it. "You hear anything, you let me know."

Zeb nodded. "Will do."

Savage turned to Lucas, who waited nearby.

"Let's head back. We've got work to do."

TWENTY-FOUR

SAVAGE SPOTTED Beckett through the station window before he even stepped inside. The mayor, Jasper McAllister, flanked him, and judging by the looks on their faces, they meant business.

The squad room went quiet as the door hissed open.

"Sheriff," Beckett called, ignoring Barb, who stood up to greet him. "We need a word."

Savage stood at the door to his office. "Come on through." He nodded at Barb, before closing the door behind them.

Turning to face them, he asked, "This about Walter Minstrel?"

"It is," McAllister replied with a curt nod. "We heard the victim was associated with the Crimson Angels."

"That is correct."

Beckett glanced at McAllister, then back to Savage. "That makes two dead. In under a week. Tied to the same club. We've got a community center full of evacuees, fire lines cutting off half the roads in and out of town, and now another homicide tied to a known outlaw organization."

Savage held his gaze. "I hope you didn't come all this way to state the obvious?"

145

"We came to say this ends now," Beckett snapped. "That club needs to be dismantled—disbanded—whatever it takes. You do whatever you have to do, but I want them gone."

Savage took a step toward them, slow and deliberate. "You want them gone, Royce? Go file a motion. Draft a proposal. Make a speech at your next city council meeting. But don't walk into my office and tell me how to do my damn job."

Beckett opened his mouth, but Savage cut him off.

"I don't tell you how to run elections. You don't tell me how to run an investigation."

McAllister raised a calming hand. "No one's questioning your ability, Sheriff. We just need to know you're taking this seriously."

"In addition to what you so helpfully pointed out, I've got a missing woman and her kid to find. None of us have slept in almost seventy-two hours. I'd say we're taking it pretty damn seriously."

Silence.

Savage held open the door, startling the rest of the team, who hastily turned away and pretended to be typing furiously. "Now, if you'll excuse me, gentlemen. I've got work to do."

"So much for our upliftment grant," Barb murmured, as they left.

"I heard that," Savage muttered, coming out of his office.

Sinclair shot Barb a warning look.

Savage raked a hand through his hair. "What the Mayor and Beckett don't understand is that if we get rid of Rosalie and the Crimson Angels, we get outsiders muscling in. Mobsters from Denver and Philly flooding our county with fentanyl, heroine and oxy. It's bad enough already but add that on top of it and you're fighting a war you just can't win. At least this way we know who we're dealing with."

Lucas absorbed this, nodding in agreement. "Rather the devil you know?"

"Exactly."

"Plus, Rosalie cooperates with us," Thorpe pointed out.

"To a point," Sinclair amended.

Savage grunted. Either way, the Angels were better than the menace that would replace them if there was a gap in the market. Right now, nobody wanted to mess with them. Hawk's Landing was their turf, and anyone who'd tried had failed. He'd helped Rosalie see to that.

"Hopefully, this'll blow over when we catch whoever killed these three men," Lucas said, glancing between them.

Savage wasn't so sure.

"Let's get back to work. What have we got on Honey Granger?

Thorpe turned away from his screen. "The fire department got back to me about her vehicle. It was deliberately set alight. There was gasoline all over the exterior, as well as inside."

Savage frowned. "Someone wanted to destroy evidence. Or erase a crime scene."

Thorpe added, "Well, they sure did that. The fire was so hot, Pearl didn't find any usable prints and no trace evidence."

"You got the samples back already?"

He nodded. "Pearl said it was easy since there wasn't anything to find."

"It's been twenty-four hours," Sinclair pointed out.

He knew what she meant. With every hour that passed, it was looking less likely they'd find them alive.

"We keep going," he said. "Until we find their bodies, they're missing, not dead."

She nodded and turned back to her screen.

Thorpe leaned back in his chair. "Why torch the car? They must know we'd find it."

"I don't know," Savage said. "That part doesn't make sense. It was left in the wildfire zone, so it would have burned anyway."

Thorpe nodded. "Maybe they didn't want to take a chance."

"Could be." Savage turned to Sinclair and Lucas. "Let's canvas the area again. Look for street cams that are still operational. Doorbell footage. Traffic intersections. Anything within a mile radius of where her vehicle was found. Someone may have seen something."

"The area was being evacuated," Sinclair reminded them. "The place was chaos, but I'll see what footage I can find."

"I'll head out there," Lucas said. "Knock on doors. Now the fire's no longer a threat, folks will be moving back home."

Thorpe stifled a yawn. "I'm looking for a transit van, people carrier, anything low key and unobtrusive. They'd have to have kept them out of sight."

Savage nodded. "Good point."

He went back to his office, but before he could close the door, Barb elbowed her way in. "Dalton, you're exhausted. You need to go home."

"I can't. Not while they're still out there."

"You can," she said firmly. "The team is on it, and I will call you if there's any news. I promise. You're crabby and short tempered, and I don't want you to fall out with any more councilmen. We've probably blown our chances with the committee as it is."

He swiped at his forehead. Barb's face swam in front of his eyes. Maybe she was right. If he didn't grab some sleep soon, he was going to fall down.

"Okay, but I'll be back later."

She nodded. "I expect nothing less."

Savage left, tiredness making him more emotional than usual. He was desperate to speak to Becca, hear her voice. He missed talking through his cases with her, brainstorming scenarios. She was always so calm and insightful. Her psychological background helped him make sense of the senseless crime he dealt with on a daily basis. Now she was gone, and all this stuff rattled around in his head unchecked.

By the time Savage pulled into Apple Tree Farm, the sky was bleeding orange and mauve. He climbed out on weary legs. An hour. That was all he needed to replenish his energy, then he could go back in and continue the search.

He looked up, blinked, and then blinked again.

Was he hallucinating?

DUST DEVIL

Exhaustion could do that to a person. He frowned, took a few steps closer, then stared at the vision on his porch.

Honey Granger sat there, her arms wrapped around her son. Ben leaned into her, clutching a toy dinosaur. His cheeks were streaked with dirt, his eyes wide and watchful.

She got to her feet, wild eyes scanning the land around them. "Sheriff, I'm sorry to just show up like this, but I didn't know where else to go."

Savage stared at her for a long moment. If she was talking, she must be real.

Her clothes were wrinkled, her face drawn. A protective hand still rested on Ben's shoulder.

"Are you okay?" he asked.

She smoothed down her dress. "Yeah. I think so. Nobody knows I'm here."

Then, he got it.

Honey had faked her own disappearance. She'd torched her car in the hopes of throwing whoever was after her and Ben off the trail. She'd even made it look like her car had been caught in the wildfire. Smart move.

"Come inside," he said, quietly. "You're safe now."

TWENTY-FIVE

SAVAGE CLOSED the front door behind them, the latch clicking softly into place. Inside the farmhouse, it was dim and quiet. He flicked on the light.

"Can I get you something? A glass of water?"

She nodded. "Water would be good."

He went to the cabinet, took down a glass, filled it and handed it over. She accepted it, bent down and helped Ben take a long drink. Then, she downed the rest. "Thank you."

He nodded and took the glass back. In the hall light, he could see how dirty their clothes were, and that their shoes were caked in soot. The familiar scent of smoke hung off both of them. A smear of ash ran across her cheek like war paint.

Savage gestured to the living room. "Come and sit down."

She hesitated, then took Ben's hand and followed him. Tentatively, she sank down onto the couch, pulling Ben up beside her. The kid still looked terrified.

"I'll be right back."

Savage hurried to a cabinet in the spare bedroom and rummaged inside until he found one of Connor's old toys, a plastic fire engine. It was scuffed and battered but intact. Returning, he bent down in front of Ben.

"Hey, buddy." He held out the toy. "You like trucks?"

Ben looked to his mother for permission. Honey gave a shaky nod, and the boy slowly reached for it.

"Thank you," he murmured.

"You're very welcome."

Savage went over to an armchair and sat down. Honey might feel more relaxed if he wasn't towering over her. "Now, why don't you tell me what happened."

Her voice was fragile. "I was on my way to drop Ben off at daycare, when I noticed a car behind me. At first, I thought I was being paranoid, but it followed me into the school parking lot and just sat there. Not moving."

Savage's jaw tensed. "Can you describe it?"

"It was an SUV. Black, with dark windows."

That didn't really narrow it down. "What about the occupants? Did you see the driver?"

"No, they didn't get out."

He frowned. "And you're sure they were watching you?"

"I wasn't at first," she admitted. "But it followed me all the way to school, even into the parking lot."

"What did it do then?"

"Nothing. It was like they were waiting for me. I got this bad feeling. You know?"

He nodded. He did know. Instinct. It was rarely wrong, but not many people listened to it. They preferred to tell themselves there was nothing to worry about, that they were just being silly. No need to make a fuss.

Except Honey hadn't done that. She'd acted.

"I couldn't risk dropping Ben off. What if they grabbed him?" She gulped and wrung her hands together. "So I took off and kept driving. I circled the block a few times and tried to lose them, but just when I thought I had, they'd pop up behind me."

He frowned. "That does confirm it."

She bit her lip. "I ditched my phone, in case they were tracking me somehow." She gave a helpless shrug. "I don't know if it helped."

He recalled that her boss had seen her with two phones, but he didn't mention it.

"Then what?"

She exhaled shakily. "I panicked. Drove out of town, toward the ridge. Toward the fire. I know it sounds crazy, but I figured... if I lost them in the smoke, maybe they'd give up. It worked. At least, I think it did. I pulled off near one of the old back roads, close to where they were evacuating people."

She looked down at Ben, who was rolling the fire truck slowly across his knees.

"I left the car there. There was ash all over the place. The fire was so close, we could feel the heat. I knew the car would catch eventually. I hoped they'd think we were still in it."

"You lit it?" Savage asked.

"No," she said quickly. "But I poured gasoline inside. There was a canister in the back from when I ran out weeks ago. I left the doors unlocked and figured it would go up on its own once the fire reached it."

He gave a slow nod. She'd figured right.

"So, how'd you get here?"

"We walked to the edge of the evacuation zone. There were residents loading their belongings into cars, kids were crying, some families were looking for their pets. It was pretty chaotic. I found a couple who were leaving and told them my husband was supposed to come and fetch us, but he couldn't get through. They believed me and dropped me here. I said you were a friend."

"Why me? We've never met. You don't know me from Adam."

"I trust you." Her voice cracked, and it moved him. "You were kind to my mom. And your deputies... they treated me like I mattered. I knew I'd be safe with you."

That landed heavily in his chest. It was why he did this job. To help people. To serve the community.

He cleared his throat. "You did the right thing."

She jumped as the wind rattled the porch screen, her head spinning to the door.

"It's okay, it does that."

Her shoulders dropped, but she glanced down at Ben, who'd slid off the couch and was now playing on the floor with the truck.

"He's everything to me," she whispered.

"You're both safe now." Savage gave a reassuring nod. "You have my word."

She exhaled, clearly relieved, but he sensed a resolve in her. Honey was a strong, resilient woman, and she'd do what she had to in order to protect her son. He could see that about her.

"Honey, do you have any idea why someone would come after you?"

"No, not really. I mean, do you think this has something to do with Dean, or the phone?"

Savage frowned. "What phone?"

She reached into her jacket and pulled out a small flip phone, scratched and dirty. It looked ancient. "I found this the other day. It was in a box of Dean's stuff."

"The other day?" Savage took it from her and studied it. That model had been popular around six or seven years ago. The only reason he knew was because he'd had a similar one back in Denver, when he was on the Force.

"Yeah. My mother stashed a box of his things in the attic after he left, but when your deputies told me what had happened, I got it down and went through it. That's when I found the phone."

It was plausible.

"Did you try to turn it on?"

She shook her head. "The battery's dead and I don't have the right charger."

"It wasn't with the rest of his stuff?"

She shook her head. "No. I don't think it was his. I've never seen it before."

Savage inspected the device, turning it over in his hand. He might have a cable lying around that would fit. Honey was smart, he'd give her that much. Her skills were wasted working at the diner.

"Okay. Well, why don't you get cleaned up and have a rest. I'm sure you and Ben are exhausted. You're more than welcome to stay here for the time being."

She gave a relieved smile. "Oh, thank you, Sheriff. That would be great."

"Do you want to call your mother? She's worried about you."

"I would, but what if they're listening to my phone calls or have tapped her phone?"

She had thought of everything.

"Don't worry, I'll send a deputy around to let her know. That way there'll be no trace."

"Thank you."

Savage rubbed his forehead, trying to think through the fog of weariness and stress. "You think the people following you were from the Crimson Angels?"

"Mm... I don't think so. I haven't seen any motorcycles outside or club members watching the house. Up until yesterday, I didn't notice anyone watching me at all."

Savage grunted. This felt too slick an operation for the Angels. They didn't drive around in tinted SUVs and snatch kids out of daycare parking lots. They were more aggressive, less covert.

He glanced down at the phone in his hand. It could just be one that Diesel used to communicate with other club members. A useless burner.

Then again, it might have something on it they could use. Something that would tell them who had killed Diesel.

But why now, when the phone had been in a box in her mother's attic for over three years.

"Honey, have you told anyone about this phone?"

She shook her head.

"And you haven't turned it on?"

"No, I told you, it's dead."

Frowning, he shoved it into his pocket. Thorpe would be able to bring it back to life, and then they could analyze the call logs.

"Why don't I show you around, and you can get cleaned up."

She got to her feet. "Your wife won't mind us staying here?"

He hesitated. "My wife isn't home at the moment, and neither is my son."

She gave an unsure nod but followed him into the hall. He showed her the spare room, the guest bathroom and the kitchen. "Make yourself at home. I have to go back to work, so you'll have the house to yourself."

She bit her lip.

"Don't be afraid," he added. "You're quite safe here. Nobody knows where you are, and they'll never think to look here for you. I won't disclose your location. Not even to my deputies. You can relax."

A shaky sigh, but he could sense the relief washing off her.

"I'll leave you be," he said, heading for the front door.

So much for catching a few hours of sleep. Strangely, he was no longer tired. The turn of events had invigorated him. It was time to head back to the office and figure out who was after Honey, and what, if anything, was on that phone.

TWENTY-SIX

BACK AT THE Sheriff's office, Savage slid the battered flip phone across the desk toward Thorpe.

"Think you can bring this thing back to life?"

Thorpe picked it up. "This is ancient. What is it, 2010?"

"Something like that. It belonged to Diesel Vaughn. Honey found it a couple of days ago in a box of his things."

"Honey?"

"Yeah, I found her. She's safe. We can cancel the BOLO."

They all turned to stare at him, while Barb put her hands on her hips. "I told you to go home."

"Where is she?" Sinclair blurted out. Lucas and Thorpe raised their eyebrows expectantly.

Savage cleared his throat. "At my place."

"Wait? Is she okay?" Sinclair stared at him. "What about her son?"

"How did she get there?" Thorpe asked, the phone still in his hand.

"Did she manage to get away?" Lucas questioned.

Savage put up his hands as if to shield himself from the barrage

156

of questions. "Everybody calm down. I got home last night, and she was sitting on my doorstep. Her and Ben. They're both fine."

"I don't understand," Barb asked, pulling out a chair and easing herself into it. "What happened?"

"Then, she wasn't kidnapped?" Lucas surmised. "She went on the run."

Savage perched on the side of Thorpe's desk. His deputy bent to rummage through a drawer of cables.

"Claimed she was being watched. A black SUV with tinted windows followed her to her son's daycare. Fearing for their lives, she panicked and went off the grid."

"How come we found her vehicle in the fire zone?" Sinclair asked.

"That was intentional. She was trying to lose her tail."

"The Crimson Angels?" Lucas asked Savage.

He gave a little shake of his head. "Doesn't appear to be, although we can't rule them out. Honey didn't get a plate, but a black SUV with tinted windows isn't their MO."

Thorpe plugged in the phone. "You're right, that doesn't sound like them." He frowned as nothing happened.

"Is it dead?" Savage asked.

After a moment, the charging light flickered to life. Thorpe smirked. "Nope, not yet. Give me a second and I might have something for you."

"Who could it be?" Sinclair leaned forward, elbows on her desk. "Is she sure the SUV was following her?"

"She's adamant. I don't think she's making it up. Her and Ben were filthy, and exhausted when I found them. And I could tell her fear was real."

Sinclair gave a thoughtful nod. "Who else would want to hurt them?"

"I wish I knew." Savage turned to Thorpe. "See what you can pull from any undamaged CCTV in the neighborhood where her vehicle was found. You're looking for a dark SUV, not a van or transporter."

"On it." He swiveled back to his computer.

Beside him, the phone's screen lit up. Thorpe picked it up, glanced at the screen, and gave a surprised snort. "No passcode, that's good."

Savage spun around. "Can you get in?"

"Working on it."

Lucas straightened up. "Shouldn't someone tell Honey's mother her daughter is safe?"

Sinclair reached for her phone. "I'll do it."

Savage glanced up. "Do it in person. We don't want to risk calling in case whoever is after Honey is bugging her mother's phone."

"Good point." She got to her feet, tucking her phone into her back pocket.

"Also, don't tell her where her daughter is, just that she's okay," Savage was quick to add. "We don't want the location getting out."

Sinclair frowned. "If someone was following Honey, is her mother safe? Maybe she should stay with a friend for a while, just until this is over."

Savage nodded. "Offer to take her. That way we'll know she's okay."

Savage turned back to Thorpe. "Find anything?"

He pursed his lips. "No contact details, no messages, no call log. Looks like it's been wiped clean."

"Damn," Savage muttered. He'd been hoping for a lead. Something that would make sense of everything, but he'd always known it was a longshot. In all likelihood, the phone had nothing to do with the people following Honey.

Thorpe made an excited sound in the back of his throat.

"What?" Savage asked.

The man broke into a grin. "There's a voice message. Whoever owned the phone forgot to delete it."

Savage felt a tiny spark of hope. "Let's hear it."

Thorpe hit play. A grainy timbre filled the squad room. He'd have to check with Honey, but he was willing to bet it was Diesel Vaughn's voice.

"You said you could handle this, and I took your word on that. Now I've got Axle breathing down my damn neck, asking questions. This money was supposed to be clean by last week. You promised there'd be no delays. I don't care how powerful you are, you don't keep Axle waiting. You got no idea what kind of heat that brings. I've done my part. You do yours."

The message cut out.

No sign-off. No name. Just a tense, urgent rasp. The speaker was anxious, in a hurry.

Lucas let out a low whistle. "Assuming that was Diesel, it didn't sound like he was talking to another biker."

Thorpe tapped the screen. "The phone is definitely a burner. It's unregistered."

"If that's Diesel's voice leaving the message, it can't be his phone," Savage muttered.

"Why did he have it in his possession, then?" Lucas asked. "Did he steal it?"

Savage ground his teeth together. "I don't know. Maybe he took it for insurance. The Angels were involved in a lot of criminal enterprises back then. Maybe Diesel, or the guy who owned the phone, was part of it."

Barb entered the room carrying a tray with mugs of coffee.

"Sounds like whoever Diesel was talking to laundered money for the Angels," she said, setting the tray down on Thorpe's desk.

Savage grunted in agreement. "But who is that?"

Lucas reached for a mug. "A businessman. Or someone in government. Maybe even law enforcement."

"Could it have been Sheriff Jeffries?" Savage accepted a mug from Barbara. "Scooter mentioned Axle had something going down with him. Could be his phone."

Barb frowned. "How would Jeffries launder the money? He didn't have access to any banking facility or small business."

That was true.

"Let's check that burner number against his phone records, and any calls made from this office landline when he worked here."

Thorpe gave a worried nod. "I can't cross-reference the burner number with any government-issued phones or landlines without a warrant."

Savage knew the protocols. "Just concentrate on Jeffries for now."

Thorpe snapped his fingers. "What about that shady banker? You know, the one we suspected was a member of that secret organization, the Guardians. He scrapped that prospective land deal last year."

Savage thought about that. Ace Reynolds was a respected bank manager at Silver Ridge Bank in Hawk's Landing. Last year, he'd claimed the sale of a farm to outside developers fell through on a technicality, but they were convinced he'd called off the sale to keep the Guardians happy.

The Guardians.

A constant thorn in his side.

They were a clandestine organization made up of prominent businesspersons, landowners, and politicians who wielded considerable sway over the county's policies and development.

"I'll pay him a visit," he said, rubbing his eyes. "He might not be directly involved, but he could know who is."

Thorpe's voice took on a faraway quality as he thought out loud. "If this man was a politician or someone with power, he could have had Diesel silenced to get him off his back, or to hide his involvement."

Lucas picked up the thread. "When Diesel's body was discovered, and we started investigating, he was worried the whole money laundering scandal would come to light again. That's why he went after Honey. He knew she had the phone."

"He could have shot Axle too," Thorpe added.

"But why now?" Savage shook his head. There were still too many what-ifs. "Why not kill him at the same time as Diesel?"

DUST DEVIL

Nobody could answer that.

Savage sighed, wishing it wasn't such a quagmire. There was no clear evidence, no proof of anything, only supposition.

And the phone message.

"We need to find out who Diesel—if that was him—was calling."

"I'll do my best," Thorpe said with a grimace. "But without a name, and no warrant, there's not much to go on."

"I know." Savage took a fortifying sip of coffee. "Thanks, Barb."

She raised her hand. "You look like you need it."

They all did.

Savage walked back to his office. It was possible Diesel had been silenced because he knew too much. And someone still wanted that secret buried.

An hour later, he called it a day. They were all in desperate need of sleep, and he didn't think there was anything more they could do tonight. Honey was safe—for now. They could pick this up again in the morning.

———

THE GLASS FAÇADE of Silver Ridge Bank shimmered in the late morning sun, its tasteful awning casting a welcome shadow across the sidewalk.

The wildfires were still smoldering, but according to Mason, who'd filed a sitrep first thing this morning, they were under control once again. Even so, the evacuation order was still in place, and the main street was filled with residents staying in the one hotel in town, and various bed and breakfasts, as well as the community center, in search of a morning coffee. A long line had formed outside the Bouncing Bean, which had never seen such a large crowd.

Inside the bank, however, there was an air of quiet efficiency as the staff and customers went about their business. Marble floors, polished counters, discreet tellers in navy jackets guiding clients through wire transfers and mortgage queries.

Savage didn't bother waiting in line. He strode straight up to the reception desk and flashed his badge. "Please tell Mr. Reynolds that Sheriff Savage is here to see him."

The receptionist blinked, startled, then gave a tight nod and lifted the phone.

Ace Reynolds appeared less than two minutes later, his tailored suit impeccable, his smile fixed and guarded.

"Sheriff." He extended a hand, but his smile did not reach his eyes. "How nice to see you."

"Is there somewhere private we can talk?" Savage asked.

The fake smile slipped. "Let's go to my office."

He led the way through the bank's back corridor, passing a row of private glass-partitioned rooms, until they reached his corner office. It was tastefully decorated with leather chairs, a tidy desk, and framed certificates on the walls.

Savage didn't sit. He waited until Reynolds had closed the door, then got straight to it. "I'm looking into a potential money laundering scandal."

Reynolds's gaze narrowed. "What makes you think my bank's involved?"

"You're the only bank in town, and the evidence I have suggests a money laundering scheme involving one or more of your customers."

"Who?"

"Former Sheriff Jeffries, who you know is incarcerated, and Axle Weston, who was murdered."

The banker's eyes widened. "Axle Weston is dead?"

Savage gave a curt nod.

Ace ran a hand over his receding hairline. "I wasn't aware... But despite that terrible tragedy, what makes you think he was involved in money laundering?"

Terrible tragedy indeed. Ace wouldn't lose a moment's sleep over the former president of the Crimson Angels' demise.

"We have evidence to that effect. I can't share it with you, but I do need your help to check on a customer who may also be involved."

"Who?"

"I don't have a name, only a phone number."

Ace stared at him for a long moment. "I'm going to need to see a warrant before I hand over any confidential customer information."

"This goes back three years."

"Even so."

Savage stepped forward, dropping his voice. "Fine. I'll get a warrant. My guys will come in here and tear through your computers. We'll seize the servers. Lock up client accounts. Your biggest investors will walk the second this place makes the news. The board will remove you before lunchtime."

Reynolds paled.

"You can't protect your client, Reynolds. I'm investigating two homicides and an attempted kidnapping. If that number is on your bank's call registry or linked to an account, I need to know. I want a name. So either you help me, or you get caught in the blast radius."

Reynolds stared at him, lips pressed in a tight line. Then he lowered himself into his chair like a man aging ten years in one breath.

"Even if I could give you that information, three years is a long time. I don't know if we even retain records—"

"It's not that long ago." Savage pinned Reynolds with his steely gaze. "All I need is a caller ID, not the actual conversation. Besides, if the number is linked to an account, or was used in a wire transfer or transaction, you'll have it in your system."

The banker shifted in his chair. "Look, Sheriff, I'd love to help you out, but nobody is using my bank to launder money. We have checks in place to prevent against that type of thing."

"It's easy to look the other way."

Ace didn't reply. If the Guardians were involved, he tended to look the other way a lot. Ace knew Savage was aware of that.

Savage pursed his lips, looking around. "The bank logs all incoming calls, doesn't it? For quality assurance and compliance reasons."

Reynolds stiffened. "Technically, yes, but I don't know how long we keep them for."

Savage slid a piece of paper with the burner phone number on it across the desk. "Could you find out? I'll wait."

Reynolds studied the note. "You want me to find out if this number ever called this office?"

"Or is tied to an account here at the bank."

Sighing, Reynolds picked up the paper, got slowly to his feet, then walked to the door. "Bear with me."

"I'll be right here."

He walked out, leaving Savage alone in his office.

Savage eyed the banker's computer, the screen still flickering in the window's reflection. He hadn't logged off. How easy would it be to nip around, check his emails, or the bank's database...?

Except he couldn't. If he got caught, that was potentially the end of his career. Certainly the end of the department's funding drive.

Tightening his jaw, he settled back to wait. This had to be by the book, or else it wouldn't stand up. If someone powerful was involved, successful prosecution would depend on whatever proof they could gather. And you could bet they'd be up against the best legal team available.

It took ten minutes, but Reynolds returned, his face set in a grim line. Savage knew the banker had the information he needed.

"You found it?" he hissed, under his breath.

Reynolds gave a hesitant nod, but said, "I'm afraid there was no mention of that number in our database."

Savage slanted his eyes. He was lying. Why?

Was he afraid his office was bugged? That someone would overhear him give the Sheriff condemning information on one of his customers?

Slowly, Reynolds slid the piece of paper back to him across the desk. Eyes downcast, he said, "Sorry I couldn't be of more help."

Savage glanced down at the note. Underneath the number, in a shaky sprawl, the banker had written one word. A name.

BECKETT.

TWENTY-SEVEN

OUTSIDE, the bank's air-conditioned chill gave way to a blast of heat as Savage stepped into the midday sun. So, Beckett was dirty. Why wasn't he surprised?

Had Beckett and Sheriff Jeffries been in it together? Had the sheriff looked the other way while Beckett laundered drug money for the Crimson Angels? Jeffries had been as corrupt as they came, so he wouldn't have done it without securing a slice of the pie for himself.

Jaw set, Savage pulled out his phone and called Thorpe. When his deputy answered, he told him what he'd discovered.

"Beckett? Really?" Thorpe spluttered on the other end of the line.

"Yeah, it was his burner that Diesel called that day, asking about the clean funds. It was Beckett who laundered the money."

"That dirty scumbag," Thorpe muttered.

Savage grunted in agreement. To think he'd groveled for the county-allocated funds. The thought made him hot under the collar.

"We'll bring him down," Savage decided, his voice tight. "We just need to prove it. The bank has a record of the caller ID and a time-stamp, but no conversation. They don't keep the recordings that long. In itself, that's not going to stand up."

"It might help sway a jury?" Thorpe insisted.

"Even so, we'll need a court order to get it. Get on the phone to Judge Mathis. As far as I know, he's a straight arrow and isn't a member of the Guardians."

Mathis was based in Durango and out of the Guardians' remit. He was also a personal friend of Sheriff Shelby, who had helped Savage's department several times over the years. If anyone would grant them a court order for something so nefarious, it would be him.

"On it," Thorpe said grimly.

"Also, start digging through Beckett's financial history. Any shell companies, unusual deposits, big donations. We need to find out how the money laundering scam worked."

"Will do."

Savage clicked off and stood still for a moment, squinting at the bank. Jeffries was currently serving an eight-year sentence at the minimum-security Arrowhead Correctional for accepting bribes in addition to knowingly violating the law and failing to perform his duty. Maybe he'd be prepared to give evidence against Beckett in return for an early release.

Savage gnawed on his lower lip. Judge Mathis would have to agree. Somehow, they'd have to get him onboard.

A little after four, Thorpe called back, frustration thick in his voice.

"Sheriff, it's a no-go on the court order."

Savage stopped mid-step on his porch. He'd gone home to see how Honey and Ben were getting on. Thankfully, they were both fine and looking a lot more rested than the day before.

"What do you mean no-go?"

"Mathis flatly refused. Said there wasn't sufficient probable cause to justify a subpoena for confidential banking communications."

Savage swore under his breath. "Did you tell him it ties Beckett to money laundering and possibly two murders?"

L.T. RYAN

"I told him everything. He said it's all circumstantial. That without solid evidence linking Beckett to the phone, the call could've been from anyone using that line. He wants more before he'll even consider signing."

Savage scrubbed a hand over his jaw. "I was afraid of this. He's being careful. He knows this has potentially far-reaching consequences. Problem is, he isn't wrong."

"Yeah," Thorpe agreed. "Or maybe someone leaned on him."

Savage pondered this. "Mathis seemed legit when I last dealt with him, although that was some time ago."

"What do you want to do, boss?" Thorpe asked.

Savage's fingers tightened around the phone. "I don't know. Yet. Give me half an hour and I'll be back in the office. We can figure out next steps then."

"Copy that," Thorpe said, before cutting the call.

"YOU THINK Jeffries will go for it?" Sinclair asked later that afternoon.

Savage paced up and down the bullpen, hands thrust deep in his pockets. "Don't know. We can try."

He was grasping at straws, but without the court order, this was his only recourse. And he knew Jeffries. There was only one thing that would get him to rat out his co-conspirators.

A deal.

Lucas glanced up. "Don't we have to go through the District Attorney's Office if we want to offer him a reduced sentence?"

His deputy was correct. Only prosecutors could offer parolees early releases in exchange for cooperation.

"I suggest we first talk to him off the record. He's going to need reassuring that nothing he says can be used against him. Then, if what he offers is useful, the DA might be prepared to negotiate a deal —on the condition that Jeffries agrees to testify against Beckett."

"You're sure he'll do that?" Sinclair queried. "Beckett is most likely a member of the Guardians. Jeffries won't want to step on their toes."

"If he doesn't, he's going back to prison to finish his eight-year sentence. So yeah, I think he might risk it."

"Worth a shot," Lucas agreed. "What have we got to lose?"

———

THE NEXT MORNING, Savage waited in a private interview room at Arrowhead Correctional Center, the kind reserved for law enforcement debriefs and pre-arranged attorney-client meetings. A corrections officer stood by the door, arms crossed, neutral but alert.

The room was cold, quiet, and bare. The only furniture was a metal table, two bolted down chairs, and a heavy security door. No glass partition, no microphones, only a camera mounted high up in the corner—for security purposes.

A moment later, former sheriff Larry Jeffries was led in, his wrists cuffed and ankles shackled. He looked older and paler that Savage remembered, but he carried himself with the same swagger he always had.

"Sheriff Savage," he drawled, glowering at Savage under the harsh fluorescent light. "To what do I owe the pleasure?"

"Have a seat," Savage said evenly.

Jeffries sat, resting his hands on the table with a metallic clink. "What's this about? You finally come to gloat? Well, you're about three years too late."

Savage kept his voice neutral. "Four, actually, but no. This is an off-the-record conversation. Nothing said here leaves this room unless you agree to make a formal statement. But if you're willing to cooperate, I can speak to the District Attorney. Possibly recommend a reduction in your sentence."

Jeffries's stiffened. "You offering me a deal?"

"I said I'd recommend it. The DA makes the deal. Not me."

A beat passed.

L.T. RYAN

Jeffries lifted his chin. "What do you want?"

"Councilman Beckett." Savage fixed his gaze on his predecessor. "We believe he was laundering money for the Crimson Angels. That he used Silver Ridge Bank to clean the cash. You were sheriff at the time. Did you know about this?"

There was a moment when Jeffries's eyes widened, just a little, but he covered it well. "I don't know what you're talking about, Sheriff. I didn't even know Councilman Beckett."

"Your phone records say otherwise," Savage said. Thorpe had managed to find several calls from the Sheriff's office to Beckett's private line. Unfortunately, not to the burner phone, and those calls in themselves were not evidence.

Jeffries snorted, but Savage could tell he was rattled. "You'll have to do better than that."

Savage leaned in slightly. "Diesel Vaughn left a voice message on a burner phone, one we know belonged to Beckett."

Jeffries looked him straight in the eye. "Who's Diesel Vaughn?"

Savage tensed. "A runner for the Angels."

He shrugged. "If you know that, why'd you need me?"

"You were complicit, Larry. If you're willing to testify against Beckett, the DA might trade that for early release. You get to walk out of here. Don't you want that?"

Jeffries's lips curled into a tight smile. "You always were a Boy Scout, weren't you, Savage?"

Savage didn't respond.

Jeffries drew in a long breath. "You think Beckett's just a guy with a seat at City Hall? He's got friends. Powerful ones. You know what that means?"

The Guardians.

"I know what it means."

"Then you know this is career suicide."

"You don't have a career." Not anymore.

A smirk. "It wasn't me I was talking about."

"I'm trying to solve a triple homicide here, Jeffries. I think I'll take

DUST DEVIL

the risk. I know that's never been your work ethic, but I was hoping the early parole might persuade you to do the right thing."

Jeffries's smile faded, but he was thinking about it. Eventually, he said, "I'd like to stay alive in here. You think someone like Beckett doesn't have reach? You think prison walls keep him out?"

Savage studied him, his heart sinking. He could read the writing on the wall. This wasn't going anywhere. Jeffries wouldn't budge. He was too scared of messing with Beckett, and by default, the Guardians.

Still, he had to know. "But you knew? You knew Beckett was dirty?"

Jeffries tensed. "Not on record, I didn't. This is a confidential discussion, right?"

Savage gave a reluctant nod.

"Okay, then. A lot of things went down when I was in office. Deals were made. Some benefited the town. Others didn't. It was in my best interests to... turn a blind eye."

"You take a cut?"

He didn't respond.

"I'll take that as a yes."

"Take it how you want. I'm not saying anything else. It doesn't matter now, anyway. It was a long time ago."

There was no statute of limitations on justice, in his book.

"It matters if you're willing to testify."

Jeffries gave a bitter laugh. "So I can go up in front of a judge and say Beckett was dirty? Then what? Spend the rest of my life looking over my shoulder?" He shook his head. "No thank you."

"Would it change your mind if I said a woman and her child's life was at stake?"

For the first time, something flickered in Jeffries's expression. Not guilt. Not fear. Maybe regret.

"Even if I did testify... what makes you think anyone would listen? The DA isn't going to stick his neck out for me. If you think you can find a judge willing to sign off on anything that touches the

171

Guardians, you're naïve. Face it, Savage. This town's not clean. Never was. And now you're stuck in the same web of lies I was."

No, he wouldn't accept that. He couldn't.

He hadn't taken this job just to roll over.

Teeth gritted, Savage said, "We still have a chance to do the right thing."

Jeffries shook his head. "That window closed a long time ago." He leaned back in the chair, eyes flat. "I'm done talking."

Savage stood, jaw tight. "Then enjoy the next four years in here. No deal. No favors. And when the time comes, I'll make sure they remember why you stayed locked up."

Jeffries didn't flinch. "You do that."

A knock on the door. The guard entered, and Jeffries stood. As he was led away, he paused once—just long enough to glance back over his shoulder.

"You can't win this one, Boy Scout."

Then he disappeared down the hallway.

TWENTY-EIGHT

BY THE TIME Savage reached the Roadhouse, dusk had melted into full darkness. Red and blue lights pulsed across the gravel lot. DEA agents swarmed the exterior, a few posted up at the front door, rifles slung, earpieces in. Black SUVs blocked the entry, their hoods still ticking with heat.

Savage parked at the edge and climbed out. Sinclair and Lucas, in the cruiser, did the same. The call from Rosalie had come in just before nine o'clock. The DEA had rocked up and were tearing the place apart.

Rosalie stood off to the side near the picnic benches, arms crossed, jaw tight. Her patched leather vest was zipped up, her hair tied back. She looked composed, but he could see the flicker of rage beneath the surface.

"About time," she huffed as he approached. "They're ripping the place to shreds."

Savage gave a curt nod. "What exactly did they say?"

"That they got a tip," she said bitterly. "Anonymous call. Said we were stashing product on the premises. The DEA came in hot, with a warrant, and turfed us out. Shut the place down."

"Let me guess. They found something."

"Yeah." She narrowed her eyes. "Bagged heroin under the floorboards in the back office. Except, here's the thing." She leaned in, so only he could hear. "We cleared the place out two weeks ago. After Axle got shot, we knew there'd be heat. I made sure there was nothing on the property. It was clean."

He frowned. "You're telling me the H was planted?"

"That's exactly what I'm saying," she snapped, then caught herself. "Dalton, I wouldn't risk the club like that. Not now. Not with everything we've already got going on."

Savage believed her. He didn't always trust her methods, but Rosalie Weston was smart, and she would protect her own. He looked toward the agents now emerging with plastic bags and sealed evidence crates.

"Leave it with me."

He strode over to an agent with her arms full and flashed his badge. Sinclair and Lucas stood by the cruiser, eyeballing the goings on. "Who's in charge?"

"Agent Calder. Over there." She nodded toward a square-jawed man in tactical gear, talking into a radio.

Savage approached. "Sheriff Dalton Savage, Hawk's Landing. Mind telling me what this is about?"

Calder looked him up and down. "Sheriff. We had a credible tip. Controlled substances were being stored on-site."

"And you found something?"

"Twenty-five vials of heroin in a marked envelope under the rear office floorboards."

Savage didn't blink. "Funny. Because this club's already been searched by the Feds. They didn't find jack."

Calder didn't flinch. "Well, we did."

Savage studied him. "Do you really think they'd be stupid enough to leave that amount of heroin on the premises?"

He shrugged. "I don't speculate. We act on intelligence."

"Well, let me speculate for you." Savage stepped closer.

"Someone wants this place shut down, and they're trying to make that happen the fastest way possible."

"Could be," Calder said. "Doesn't mean the drugs aren't real."

"Oh, the drugs are real all right," Savage said. "They're just not theirs."

Calder said nothing. Behind him, an agent stretched police tape across the porch.

Scooter's voice cut through the silence. "Come on, man."

Calder stood up straighter. "We're shutting the bar down, pending an investigation."

Savage walked back to Rosalie. Her jaw was clenched, but she didn't argue. Instead, she met his gaze, eyes burning with frustration.

"I've got nothing to hide," she hissed. "I'm not letting them pin this on me."

Savage lowered his voice. "They won't. If the drugs were planted, there'll be no prints. No DNA. No credible link. They won't be able to make it stick."

"Dalton, I can't run the club with the Roadhouse closed."

"No," he said, leaning in towards her. "But you can help me make sure whoever did this doesn't get away with it."

Rosalie tilted her head. "You know who did this?"

"Yeah, I do." He held her gaze. "Beckett and the mayor have been to see me several times about the club. They want it gone."

"But why? What's it got to do with them?"

He hesitated, then glanced at the DEA agent standing a few yards away, out of earshot. "Apart from looking good, Beckett used to launder drug money for Axle in return for a kickback, of course."

"The dirty bastard," she hissed, her hands fisting at her sides.

"Yeah. Sheriff Jeffries was in on it too, and Diesel was the runner. It resurfaced when his body was found. Now Beckett's cleaning house."

She drew in a long breath. Her eyes glittered in the neon lights. "And they call us criminals."

He smirked.

Rosalie met his gaze. "What do you want from me?"

"Help me end this," he said quietly. "Together, we can take Beckett down. Jeffries won't testify. He's too scared of the Guardians. Axle's dead. I've got a mother and child in hiding because they know stuff they shouldn't. And your club is always going to be a target."

The silence stretched out between them. The only sound was the rustle of the tarp and muted voices as the DEA agents packed up their gear.

Then she gave a terse nod. "All right, Sheriff. I'm in. Tell me what you want me to do."

TWENTY-NINE

TOWN HALL WAS quiet the next morning when Savage stepped through the front door. He walked up to the receptionist and forced a smile. This was going to be interesting.

"I'm here to see Councilman Beckett."

She hesitated. "Do you have an appointment?"

He set his badge on the desk. "I don't need one."

"I'm sorry, Sheriff. He's very busy today. Let me see if—"

"I won't be long." Savage took off down the hallway, his strides too long for her to keep up.

Beckett's office sat at the far end of the corridor, a polished brass plaque shimmering on the door. Savage didn't bother knocking, he just opened the door and stepped inside.

"Sheriff, please—" the receptionist called after him, but it was too late.

Councilman Beckett was at his desk, reading glasses perched low on his nose, fingers tapping at a sleek wireless keyboard. He looked up, cool and composed despite the sudden interruption.

"I'm sorry, sir," the receptionist blustered. "He just walked right in."

"That's all right, Penny." He gave her a nod that said, *I've got this.*

Not for long, Savage thought, as he closed the door on a flustered Penny. When he turned back, Beckett was looking at him with an amused expression. "What's so urgent, Sheriff? I hope it's good news."

"I'm afraid not," Savage replied, moving into the center of the room. The décor was masculine and expensive. The kind of place someone decorated to remind others how powerful they were. "The Roadhouse on the Durango Road was raided last night by the DEA. They said they were acting on a tip-off. You know anything about that?"

"I heard." Beckett folded his hands neatly in front of him. "Although I can't say I'm surprised. That's what they do, those outlaw bikers. They peddle drugs, weapons and anything else they get their grubby hands on. They need to be stopped."

Savage kept his temper under control, but only just. "I don't suppose you, or a certain organization you belong to, had anything to do with it?"

Beckett's eyes narrowed. "I don't know what you're talking about."

"Of course you don't."

Beckett got to his feet. "Sheriff, if you're implying—"

"They planted heroine under the floorboards," Savage interjected. "The entire raid was orchestrated to shut down the bar."

"Now just one minute." Beckett scowled so hard his forehead funneled. "You're accusing the DEA of planting evidence?"

"That's exactly what I'm saying."

Beckett shook his head. "Be careful, Sheriff. That is a very serious accusation."

"It's a very serious crime. Heads could roll if it proves to be true."

"The tip-off was real. The DEA got the call from their anonymous tip line. You know how it works. When someone says drugs, we don't ignore it."

"Unless you're gaining from it. Isn't that right, councilor?"

DUST DEVIL

To his surprise, Beckett burst out laughing. The sound grated on him. "Are you inferring I'm involved in a drug smuggling operation?"

Savage just glared at him.

"That's ridiculous, Sheriff. Even for you. I'm merely taking the opportunity to clean up our streets. The Roadhouse has been a blight on the town for years, the mayor will attest to it. Maybe now it'll finally shut down for good."

Savage stepped forward, anger giving his voice a serrated edge. "That bar was clean. The Feds searched it a week ago. Someone planted those drugs and tipped off the DEA. They went in hot, knowing what they were going to find, and probably where they were going to find it."

Beckett's smile didn't falter. "From where I'm sitting, the DEA conducted a legitimate search and found the drugs on Rosalie Weston's property. Your MC friends have always operated on the wrong side of the law. This time, they will pay for it."

"It was a setup," Savage argued, frustration boiling up inside.

Don't say anything you'll regret, he told himself.

"To hide your part in the money laundering scheme cooked up by Axle Weston?"

Too late.

It was out there before he could take it back.

Shit. Barb was going to kill him.

They stared at each other. Neither blinked.

Beckett's smile turned glacial. "You're making a lot of noise about nothing, Sheriff. If I were you, I'd think carefully about where I spend my energy. I know I promised your department emergency funding, but I can quite easily revoke that."

"It's long overdue funding, councilor, not emergency funding. And if you're threatening my department, that might be construed as blackmail."

"I'll remind you not to tell me how to do my job," Beckett said smoothly, standing up and moving past him to open the door. "Just

179

like you told me last week. Now, if you don't mind, I have work to do."

Savage's jaw twitched, but he didn't move. It was crunch time. He'd gone too far to turn back now.

"Here's the thing, Beckett. I know you laundered money for the Crimson Angels. I've got Diesel Vaughn's voice on your burner phone, pleading for the funds to be cleaned."

For the first time, Beckett's brow twitched.

"What burner phone?" he hissed. "I've never owned a burner phone in my life."

"Rosalie Weston would disagree. She's heard the message. Diesel left the phone with her for safekeeping before he disappeared."

Before he was murdered.

"And she said I was on the message?" He closed the door again, quietly.

"Not you. Diesel Vaughn. But he was talking to you."

Beckett exhaled, clearly relieved. "Unless you can link that phone to me, it proves nothing."

"We're working on that," Savage said. "I think it'll be enough to get a judge's attention. We're going to submit it into evidence once Rosalie hands it over. Let the press run wild. Subpoena records. Interview old associates. Might even get the DA involved."

"Good luck," Beckett snapped. "But don't come crying to me when this town turns on you. When your funding dries up, when you can't protect the people closest to you, you will have me to thank."

Savage met his stare. "Another threat? Seems I've touched a nerve, councilman."

Beckett's nostrils flared.

Savage turned to go, his hand resting on the doorframe. "I'll see you in court."

He walked out without looking back, leaving the heavy silence, and a visibly rattled Beckett, behind.

. . .

DUST DEVIL

"IT'S ALL SET UP," Savage told Rosalie later that night. Once again, she'd come to Apple Tree Farm. Alone.

Nobody else knew of their ruse, and it was essential they kept it that way.

She gave a slow nod, black hair spilling sleekly from beneath her helmet. She straddled a brand-new Harley-Davidson Low Rider ST, matte black.

"Good."

He let his gaze drift over the bronze trim, the pipes gleaming in the porch light. "Nice motorcycle."

She grinned. "Thanks. Got tired of waiting for you guys to give me my old one back."

This model was leaner and meaner than her last. No tassels, no cream fender, just matte metal and muscle. Perfect for the president of an outlaw biker club.

He'd told Honey to stay out of sight. Not to let herself be seen from any of the windows. Not because he didn't trust Rosalie, but it might raise unwanted questions. He'd promised to keep her and Ben safe, no matter what.

He stepped down off the porch, so his voice didn't carry. "You can expect a raid at your house. They might try to tie it to the Roadhouse bust. Or maybe a break-in, if they're keeping it off the record. If I were you, I'd go away for a couple days. You don't want to be in the firing line."

"Noted." Her voice was cool, but the muscles in her jaw ticked. "With the Roadhouse shut, we've moved operations elsewhere."

She didn't say where. He didn't ask.

It was better if he didn't know.

"We've got deputies watching your property and the bar. Beckett will come after that phone—I'm sure of it. It's the only thing that can tie him to this."

"Even though it doesn't?"

"He doesn't know that."

Her lips curled. "That's why I like doing business with you, Dalton. You're almost as sneaky as I am."

"I doubt that," he said, half-smiling. "But thank you."

She glanced toward the farmhouse, where soft light glowed from the windows. "No drink tonight?"

"Sorry, I'm busy."

Her brow quirked. "She's back, then? That's good."

"Becca's not back."

Rosalie's smile tugged wider, slow and knowing. "You, Sheriff, are a dark horse."

"It's not like that."

"Mm..." She gave him a look, half amusement, half challenge. "You do know this little plan of yours could backfire. These are powerful men you're poking."

"They might be powerful," he said, "but they're still just men."

"Let's hope you're right." She swung one leg over her seat, settling deeper into the saddle. "I want my bar back. And I want Beckett and his lapdog agents off my ass."

"That's the idea," he said with a nod.

She gave a mock salute. "Stay safe, Sheriff. I'd hate to lose you. I'm actually starting to enjoy our... friendship."

"I wouldn't call it that."

She laughed. "Arrangement, then."

He snorted. "You stay safe too, Rosalie."

With a wink, she revved the engine. "Always."

And then she was gone—taillight flashing down the gravel drive, black hair streaming behind her like a banshee.

THIRTY

THE STREET WAS SILENT. Not the kind of small-town quiet that settled after bedtime, but the taut, expectant kind that came just before something erupted.

Savage sat in the back of a plain white delivery van, Lucas beside him. They both stared at the grainy night-vision feed mounted to the dashboard. The visuals were from a camera perched discreetly in a tree across from Rosalie's house. The screen bathed the interior, along with their faces, in a low, greenish glow.

Rosalie's place looked exactly as it should. Empty.

There were no lights in the windows, no motorcycles parked in the driveway, no cars outside. The two chairs on the porch were unoccupied, abandoned in the glow of the porch lamp.

Savage stretched his neck, trying to ease the tension in his muscles. They'd been here for hours, waiting for something to happen. The van was parked half a block away, unnoticeable unless you were looking for it.

Lucas hadn't moved much, true to his military roots. The guy had the patience of a field sniper. Savage admired his rigid spine, the way his eyes remained fixed on the screen. Savage couldn't tell what he was thinking, but his stillness spoke volumes.

He wasn't in the mood for chitchat anyway.

Sinclair and Thorpe were staking out the Roadhouse, now off-limits to the bikers, along with everyone else. They'd set up across the road, since the DEA had posted a guard, some bored sentry, to stand outside the run-down bar.

Savage didn't think Beckett would try to break in there. Not since they'd already raided the place. Any phones found on the premises had already been confiscated.

Around three AM, the hum of an engine broke the quiet. Both men turned to peer out of the front windshield as headlights appeared at the far end of the street. The vehicle approached like a shark circling its prey.

"They're casing the street," Savage murmured, as the lights got brighter. "Checking for surveillance."

Lucas gave a knowing nod as the SUV crept past, then kept going. "Recon pass."

"It'll be back," Savage murmured, as it disappeared behind the bend.

They fell silent, watching the screen, listening for the sound of an engine, or footsteps on the asphalt. The minutes stretched out like a taut elastic band ready to snap.

Then... movement.

Savage spotted them first. Two figures emerging from the brush, dressed in black, creeping stealthily toward Rosalie's property.

"They don't look like DEA agents," Lucas murmured.

"It's not Beckett either," Savage confirmed. "Must be hired muscle."

"Armed." Lucas nodded to the screen. Both men carried pistols fitted with suppressors. His hand settled on the grip of his holstered sidearm.

"One's peeling off," Savage noted, as the first man skirted the side of the house and disappeared around back. The second stopped in front, melting into the shadow of a large fir tree.

"Ready?" Savage whispered.

In response, Lucas pulled open the van door, and they ran silently, in a crouching position, toward Rosalie's house. They got there in time to hear a soft crack, barely audible, but unmistakable.

"Back window," Savage muttered, as they ducked down behind the neighbor's hedge. The street was still empty, houses in darkness. Nobody was around at this hour of the morning.

They heard the front door creak open. The second intruder darted from the shadows and entered the house. Lucas, weapon drawn but held low, turned to Savage, waiting for the command.

Savage looked him in the eye and gave a terse nod. "Let's move in."

Lucas circled the perimeter to intercept the thug who went in through the back, while Savage made his way toward the front door. No words were uttered. They didn't need them.

The night was thick and still, the lingering smoke more noticeable out here, closer to the ridge.

The thugs had left the front door ajar.

First mistake.

That told Savage these weren't seasoned pros, they were amateurs.

He pushed it wider with his foot, and sidearm drawn, finger off the trigger but ready, crept inside.

Slowly, he ventured down the hallway toward the living room. A dark silhouette searched under the sofa, his movements desperate and rushed. Savage watched as the intruder upended the large cushions on the floor. He was so involved in what he was doing, he didn't even consider that someone might have followed them in.

Second mistake.

Savage closed in. With a sudden rush, he crossed the final few feet and grabbed the man by the collar, yanking him backward.

The thug let out a strangled curse, flailing. One hand shot toward his waistband, reaching for the gun.

"Don't!" Savage barked, driving his forearm into the man's back and slamming him face-first against the wall. A dull thud echoed through the house.

But the guy wasn't going down easy. He twisted, elbowing Savage in the ribs, trying to break free. Savage grunted, muscles tightening. The man managed to turn, yanking a compact handgun from his waistband.

Too late.

Savage struck the man's wrist, sending the pistol clattering across the floor. Then he grabbed the guy's shirt and threw him sideways, using his momentum to send him crashing face-first onto the cushionless sofa.

"Hands behind your back!" Savage barked, knee in the man's spine.

The guy writhed under him, cursing again, but the fight was gone. Savage wrestled his arms backwards and slapped on the cuffs.

"Third mistake," he muttered, breath steady as he yanked the man to his feet. "You came into my town."

The thug glared at him, panting. Savage shoved him toward the front door where Lucas, not remotely out of breath, was already hauling the other intruder down the porch steps.

Outside, the sky was just beginning to pale at the edges. Soon, dawn would be creeping toward the horizon like a slow-burn fuse.

"Let's take these two back to the jailhouse," he said, eyes hard. "And see what they have to say."

Lucas gave a rare grin. "Sure thing, Sheriff."

THIRTY-ONE

SAVAGE WALKED down the narrow corridor toward Interview Room 1. He and Lucas had booked the two suspects early this morning for unlawful entry, possession of unlicensed firearms, and attempted obstruction of justice.

The statutory 24-hour clock was ticking, but they still had some time before they had to charge or release the men. Now, with the suspects stewing in the holding cells and Beckett likely doing the same in his plush Town Hall office, it was time to apply some pressure.

Savage entered the interview room and threw a manilla folder down on the steel table. The suspect was in his late twenties, jittery as hell, with a prison buzz cut and knuckles bruised from punching his way through the back window. His wrists were cuffed to the table, ankles shackled to the floor bolts. Lucas had seen to that.

He wasn't talking, but he looked scared.

Good. That was the point. Anything to make their job easier.

Savage pulled up a chair and sat down. He was calm, measured. He didn't issue any threats, just sported a serious look that said, "I mean business."

"Name?" he asked.

The guy didn't reply.

Savage sighed. "We have your fingerprints and DNA."

"Reggie," he said sourly.

"You got a last name, Reggie?" Savage asked.

"Buckland."

Savage gave a nod and opened the folder. He pulled out a black and white photograph. It was a still taken from the camera across the road from Rosalie's house. In it, you could clearly see the two men crossing the street, their weapons drawn. A bright green digital timestamp was printed in the lower right corner. It read 03:07.

Savage tapped the leaner guy on the left. "That's you, right?"

The man's eyes widened, but he didn't respond.

Savage flipped to the next image, this time of the SUV driving past the house. He turned it around so the suspect could see it more clearly. "Recognize this vehicle, Reggie?"

The man paled, the veins protruding in his scrawny neck.

Savage sat back, watching him. "We've got your vehicle casing the house at 02:43. We've got your DNA from the broken window. You want me to keep going?"

Still, the guy said nothing. His jaw clenched, but his eyes flicked to the photos. He was listening.

Savage leaned in, his voice quiet but firm. "We know why you were there. You're going down for B&E anyway. You may as well try to lighten the load by telling us who sent you."

The man hesitated. A flicker of something passed behind his eyes. Fear? Regret?

But then he shook his head. "I want a lawyer."

Savage stood, collected the photos without a word, and walked out.

———

NEXT DOOR, Sinclair faced Thug Two, who sat slouched in the metal chair, breathing heavily, a split lip already swelling from the scuffle with Savage. He was bigger than the first guy, muscular and broad-shouldered, but right now he looked like he'd rather be anywhere else but here.

She got straight to the point.

"Your buddy, Reggie, talked," she said coolly, dropping into the seat across from him. "He's cutting a deal with the Sheriff right now."

He blinked. "No, he's not."

"He is. He's already confirmed the job, the location, and the man who sent you. You want to guess how many years that's going to save him?"

He stared at her. "Bullshit."

Sinclair shrugged. "Think what you want. But you've got maybe twenty minutes before we don't need anything else from you."

He shifted in his seat.

Sinclair leaned forward, voice lower now. "So what's it going to be? You want your partner walking free while you take the rap? Full conspiracy charge, plus attempted breaking and entering, illegal possession, intent to obstruct justice..."

"No," he said quietly.

"Then talk. Let's start with your name."

His lips parted, but he still hesitated.

She gave him a long look. "You know we already know what went down, right? We know about the phone. This is your one chance to tell your side of the story. If you don't, you're liable to take the full brunt of the law."

He raised a hand. "Okay, okay."

"Okay, what?"

"I'll tell you everything."

She nodded, then looked into the camera poised above the table. "I'm listening."

"Name's Miller. Miller Stiles."

"Okay, Miller. Talk me through it."

"It was a paid job," he began, his voice halting. "We got a call from a guy we'd worked for a couple of times before. He always paid well, so we thought, why not? Sounded easy enough."

"This guy have a name?"

"Conrad. I don't know his last name."

Sinclair frowned. "How'd he contact you?"

"Called me."

She nodded. Both their cell phones were already logged into evidence. Amateurs. They'd brought them along to a break-in. Not only did the GPS data place them at the scene, but now Thorpe could pull every incoming call and trace the number that gave the order.

"What did he say?"

"He told us the house would be empty, and it would be a simple job. Five grand each, if we could find what he was looking for."

"Which was?" Sinclair waited.

"The phone, man. An old-style flip phone."

Bingo.

"What was the arrangement with Conrad?" she asked. "You know, once you'd found the phone."

"We were to call him once we had it. To arrange the handover."

"I see." She glanced up into the camera again. A few moments later, her phone beeped. Glancing down, she saw it was a message from Savage.

Set it up.

She smiled. "Miller, how'd you like to show the judge that you cooperated with us to bring down Conrad? Might make him go easy at your sentencing."

It didn't take Miller long to decide. The big shoulders shrugged. "Why the hell not. I'm screwed anyway."

THIRTY-TWO

SAVAGE HELD out Miller's phone. "Take it. I want you to call Conrad and tell him you've got the flip phone."

Miller stared at him, confused. "But I haven't."

"That doesn't matter. You want to be seen cooperating, right?"

"Yeah, man. Jeez." Miller took the phone. Scrolling through the numbers, he came to one with the initials CRD.

Thorpe had worked that one out in under five seconds. It too, was a burner, but that was to be expected. Even now, Thorpe was trying to trace its location.

Miller glanced up, and Savage gave a nod of encouragement. "Go ahead. Act like all's going according to plan. Set up the handover. Keep it on speaker."

Miller swallowed, then made the call.

When the person on the other end answered, he said, "Yeah, it's Miller. We have what you want."

The curt voice said, "You've got the device?"

It wasn't Beckett. Savage suppressed his disappointment. This was just the beginning. They'd flush him out.

"Yes, sir."

"Great. Bring it to me at the same place as before. You remember the address?"

"The warehouse? Yeah, I got it."

"Be there in an hour."

The line went dead.

Miller looked up. "How was that?"

"That was good, Miller. You did real good."

The thug gave a small shrug. "This going to help my case?"

"Yep," Savage said standing up. "The judge will take this into consideration."

"LET'S MOVE," he told his team a short while later.

They'd run a quick op's briefing in the squad room and everyone knew their role. Lucas led Miller, still cuffed, to the waiting SUV.

"You're driving," Savage said, fixing the suspect with a cold stare. "But one twitch out of line, and I will put you down. Understood?"

Miller gave a tight, resentful nod. There was no bargaining his way out of this. His buddy, Reggie, was still in the holding cell waiting for his lawyer.

The drive out to the warehouse took close to thirty minutes. Lucas sat up front with Miller, while Savage and Sinclair hunkered down in the back. The site was several miles out of town, near the Southern Ute reservation.

Once an agricultural distribution center, judging by the signage on the way there, the place had long since fallen into ruin. The weathered exterior was mottled with rust, its corrugated siding bowing from decades of desert wind. It stood alone in a sprawl of overgrown scrub and red dust, isolated and forgotten.

Half a mile out, Savage raised a hand. "Stop here."

Lucas jumped out, slinging his rifle over one shoulder as he trotted off into the brush. He'd cover them from a distance, using the Remington 700 with suppressor and optic. If things went sideways, Lucas was their ace in the hole.

DUST DEVIL

"Damn dirt," Sinclair muttered as they turned onto the access road, the tires spitting gravel. The SUV's dust plume trailed behind them like smoke from a wildfire. No way they wouldn't be seen coming.

They pulled into the lot. The loading bays out front were choked with tumbleweeds, their ramps cracked and sunken. Any windows that had been smashed were boarded with splintered plywood. A sagging chain-link fence circled the perimeter, but it had been cut through years ago and hung off worn wooden poles.

They rolled to a stop in front of the warehouse. From the opposite direction, a sleek black Mercedes appeared in the distance, carving a line through the desert like a predator on patrol. They tracked its approach by the dust it kicked up.

"Here comes Conrad," Savage murmured, under his breath.

Miller shifted in the driver's seat.

"Easy," Savage warned him.

"Where's Thorpe?" Sinclair asked from the back seat. Their presence was obscured by the tinted glass.

"In position."

Thorpe, having left before them, was already inside the warehouse. A former trail endurance racer, he'd biked out ahead and was hopefully hidden inside, rifle ready with his eyes on the entry points.

"You think Beckett will show?"

"He'll be here," Savage muttered. "He won't let someone else handle a threat like this. Not when his own neck's on the line."

He hoped he was right.

"He's going to lose his shit when he realizes we've tricked him," Sinclair murmured.

"That's the plan." Savage couldn't wait to see the look on the councilor's face. "He deserves it."

The Mercedes stopped in front of them, engine idling.

"Don't move until I say," Savage hissed from his position behind Miller. "Any sudden gestures, and it's lights out."

Miller grunted.

From the passenger side of the Merc, a broad-shouldered man with olive skin and a prominent nose stepped out. Was this Conrad? He had a gun shoved in his waistband and wore a tight tactical jacket.

"That's him," Miller murmured.

"Okay. Go give him the flip phone," Savage said.

Miller climbed out, clutching the burner in his hand. He walked slowly toward Conrad, who watched him approach, feet planted wide, weapon ready. Savage was willing to bet he was Beckett's personal enforcer. Probably a merc.

Savage scanned the Mercedes for movement, but the back seat windows were blacked out.

Come on, Beckett. Show yourself.

Miller reached Conrad. The exchange was quick. Nobody spoke.

Conrad popped the flip phone open, checked the model number, then nodded once. The rear door of the Mercedes swung open, and Beckett stepped out.

Savage broke into a grin. "Gotcha."

Beckett took the phone, tapped through a few screens, then gave Conrad a nod. "It's the right one. Take care of him and let's go."

Savage pushed his door open and stepped out, weapon drawn and levelled at Beckett. Sinclair flanked him, aiming her Glock at his center mass.

"I wouldn't celebrate just yet," Savage called.

All heads turned.

Beckett glared at him. "You set me up?"

"Afraid so."

Conrad's hand holding his weapon twitched.

"I wouldn't," Thorpe called, stepping out of the warehouse with his sidearm trained on Conrad. "We've got the whole place covered."

Miller, the only person without a firearm, backed up nervously toward Savage.

"You're done, Beckett," Savage said. "Your thugs are in custody. Both flipped on you. We've got the burner message, and now we've got you here to collect it. That's a nice little conspiracy to commit obstruction charge."

Beckett's mouth twisted. "I don't think so."

Savage's instincts spiked. He turned and saw four armed men emerging from the brush, automatic weapons trained on them.

"Shit," he hissed.

Beckett smirked. "Seems I outmaneuvered you, Sheriff. You really should stick to traffic stops. This is the big leagues."

Savage didn't blink. Neither did Thorpe. Or Sinclair. But the numbers were tight. Four bad guys versus three of them.

"Put your weapons down," Beckett ordered.

"And then what?" Savage asked, his arm steady. "You think no one will know? You think the FBI won't get curious when we all disappear?"

"Not if it looks like a turf war. You were trespassing on tribal land. Tragic accident. Hostilities with the locals. The media will eat it up."

Savage exhaled slowly. It was a good plan. Plausible. It might even have worked, except for one thing.

"You made one mistake," he said coldly. "You went after the wrong people."

"You're talking about Honey Granger?" Beckett sneered. "Turns out I didn't need her. Thanks to you, I found out Rosalie Weston had the phone. I should have known that bitch would double-cross me, just like she did her husband."

"Ex-husband," came a calm, female voice.

Rosalie stepped out of the shadows behind the warehouse.

Beckett's eyes widened in surprise.

She carried a lethal-looking assault rifle, which she'd aimed squarely at Beckett. "Call off your dogs."

Beckett turned back to Savage. "You've got to be kidding me—"

"Guess again," Savage said as Scooter emerged, followed by half a dozen of the Crimson Angels, all armed. The outlaws surrounded the mercenaries, guns pointed with deadly intent.

L.T. RYAN

"Who's the bitch now?" Rosalie said coolly.

Three of the mercs immediately dropped their rifles. The fourth hesitated, locked in a stare with Savage.

"You want to die today?" Savage asked. "Because I've got a sniper in the brush with a red dot on your forehead. You're not making it out of here if you so much as blink wrong."

The merc lowered his weapon.

"Smart choice. Toss it over there."

He did, and only then did Savage holster his Glock and move forward. He cuffed Beckett, while Sinclair secured Conrad. None of the others moved.

Only when Lucas emerged from the brush with zip ties for the mercs did the bikers back off.

"We'll need some assistance," Thorpe said, nodding to the group of thugs.

Savage led Beckett toward the SUV. "You call Tomahawk?"

"Already on his way."

Ten minutes later, three tribal police trucks rumbled into the clearing. Deputy Chief Tomahawk stepped out of the first one and looked around. "Shit, Savage. What am I walking into?"

"Your favorite kind of mess," Savage said with a grin. "Councilor Beckett and his private army were about to stage a multiple homicide and blame it on you and your guys."

Tomahawk's face darkened. "You want us to take them in?"

"Please."

Tomahawk signaled to his men. The four mercs were loaded into the trucks. Beckett, red-faced and fuming, was shoved into the back seat of Miller's SUV, flanked by Lucas and Sinclair. Thorpe drove, with Savage in the passenger seat.

As the cavalcade headed back to Hawk's Landing, Savage glanced at Beckett in his rearview mirror. "You think this is the big leagues? I'm from Denver. This is a walk in the park. And just for the record, no one messes with my town and gets away with it."

196

THIRTY-THREE

THE DOOR to Interview Room 2 closed with a quiet, deliberate click.

Savage stood inside, letting the silence stretch. Beckett sat at the table, hands cuffed in front of him, suit jacket long gone, tie askew. In the harsh, fluorescent light, he looked rumpled, angry and defeated.

Savage sat down opposite him and began the proceedings. "Name for the record?"

Beckett didn't answer.

Savage gave him a long, cool look. "I can keep you in processing for the next seventy-two hours. You won't sleep, you won't eat anything, and you sure as hell won't enjoy the company. Or, you can talk now."

"Richard Beckett," the councilor mumbled, through clenched teeth.

"Good. Now let's talk about the money. Three years ago, you laundered drug profits for the Crimson Angels. Is that right?"

Beckett stared at the table. He reminded Savage of a sulky kid in the principal's office. No problem, he could wait.

Beckett finally lifted his chin. "Yeah. I admit I helped launder drug money for Axle Weston."

Savage gave a tight nod. Now they were getting somewhere. Beckett wasn't a fool. He knew it was in his best interests to cooperate. "Walk me through it."

"It started six years ago. Axle needed clean cash, and I had the connections. Zoning permits, development funds, campaign budgets, donations. It wasn't hard to make it look legitimate."

"What did you get out of it?"

"Ten percent. Sometimes twelve."

A nice little side hustle.

"How did Diesel Vaughn fit into this?"

"Diesel was the middleman. He sold the drugs, brought me the funds, and I cleaned them. It worked well for months, until that whore came onto the scene." His lips curled back in a snarl.

Savage quirked an eyebrow. "I take it you mean Honey Granger?"

He nodded.

"Answer for the tape."

"Yes, Honey Fucking Granger."

Gone was the cool, calm politician. Instead, Beckett was reduced to a foul-mouthed scumbag. Funny how an arrest always revealed the truth. Being trapped brought out the animal instinct. Men and women reduced to their primitive nature.

"Diesel wanted out. Axle told me they wanted to run off and get married, or some such nonsense."

"And you couldn't allow that?" Savage surmised.

"I couldn't give a shit," he said. "Although, I must admit, the kickbacks were good."

"So then...?"

"It was Axle. He wanted Diesel to keep doing what he was doing. They were making money, getting rich."

Savage frowned.

Beckett was on a roll now, so Savage let him talk.

"Axle was skimming off the top, I guarantee it. The motorcycle club didn't see half of what they were making."

Now that was interesting.

He wondered what had happened to the money. Axle hadn't had much to his name when he'd been arrested. Unlike Rosalie, he wasn't financially savvy. There were no shell companies, no off-shore trusts.

"Are you saying Axle Weston shot Diesel?"

He shrugged. "All I know is I had nothing to do with it."

Savage contemplated this. How convenient for Beckett to blame a man who couldn't defend himself.

"You didn't think it strange when Diesel suddenly disappeared?"

"None of my business. My agreement was with Axle. When Diesel stopped delivering the cash, I didn't ask questions."

Savage drew in a breath. Did he believe him? He wasn't sure. Beckett must have sensed his indecision because he said, "I've never killed anyone in my life. You've got to believe me, Dalton."

Savage snorted at the false plea. "You were prepared to kill me and my team out at the warehouse."

Beckett stiffened. "That was an act of desperation."

Yeah, right.

"What about Rosalie Weston?" Savage continued. "You sent those two thugs to break into her place to get the phone. They were armed with silencers. What if she'd been home? Were they going to take care of her? Make it look like someone from the club had killed her? A bitter rival, perhaps?"

Beckett pressed his lips together.

Savage shook his head. "That's what I thought."

Beckett spread his hands. "All I wanted was that goddamn phone. I thought it would implicate me in the money laundering."

"It does."

He grimaced and folded his hands over his chest. "But that's all you've got on me?"

"That's just the beginning. You also attempted to kidnap Honey

Granger. It was Miller's SUV that followed her to her kid's school. We have police footage to prove it, backed up by CCTV."

Beckett scowled at him. "It's all circumstantial."

"Not from where I'm sitting."

"I wouldn't have hurt her or her kid," he grumbled.

Savage didn't believe him. Beckett was a brute, through and through. He might wear smart clothes, work at Town Hall, and live in a fancy mansion, but he was just a corrupt, ruthless criminal with no regard for human life. Or his responsibilities as a civil servant.

Still, all they had him on was racketeering, conspiracy, and attempted kidnapping. He couldn't charge Beckett with murder.

THIRTY-FOUR

"YOU THINK he's telling the truth?" Sinclair asked as Savage strode back into the bullpen. The team had been watching the interview on the live feed.

He clawed a hand through his hair. "I don't know. He might not have shot anyone, but that doesn't mean he wasn't complicit in their murders."

Lucas leaned against his desk, arms crossed. "Could've just hired someone to do the dirty work."

"It is possible Axle Weston killed Diesel," Sinclair said, pacing up and down as she thought. "I mean, what Beckett said was true. We know Diesel wanted out. We know he wanted to be with Honey, and that she was pregnant with his child. If Axle didn't want him to leave, he could easily have shot him and disposed of his body in the lake."

"That makes sense," Thorpe agreed with a nod. "Axle had far more to lose from Diesel quitting than Beckett did."

"Okay, let's assume that's true." Savage looked between them. "Then who killed Axle?"

"It could have been one of Beckett's thugs," Sinclair said, coming to a stop in front of him. "Once Axle was out of prison, he became a threat. If he'd been caught, there's no telling what he might have said to cut a deal."

Savage wasn't buying it. He shook his head. "Axle wasn't the type to cut a deal. He'd have gone down guns blazing rather than surrender to the marshals."

A beat passed while they contemplated this.

"Okay, then who?" Sinclair raised her hands.

Thorpe took a deep breath. "I know we've ruled her out, but I still think the only logical suspect is Rosalie."

"She did have the most to lose," Lucas agreed, nodding at Thorpe. "Axle threatened her, he damaged her reputation and almost turned her men against her. I haven't known Rosalie for long, but I'm guessing that would have pissed her off."

Savage frowned. "That's all true, but we saw the CCTV footage of her and Joel on the way to her house the night he died. Their phones pinged at that location. They were there, just like she said. Besides, she's not reckless. Shooting Axle and leaving her Harley at the scene —" He shook his head. "I don't see it."

"Could they have left again, without us knowing?" Lucas asked, clearly not wanting to give up on his theory just yet. It was a valid point.

"Not without passing through a camera," Thorpe said, adjusting his glasses.

"What about Walter Minstrel?" Savage said, his brain suddenly swirling with a fledgling idea.

Sinclair frowned. "What about him?"

He had no idea where he was going with this, but he kept talking. "Walter betrayed Rosalie. It was him, along with Rourke and Skully, who broke Axle out of prison. Maybe she asked him to make amends."

"By shooting Axle?" Sinclair gasped. "No way. He worshipped him."

Thorpe tapped his pencil on the desk while Lucas narrowed his eyes. "Unless they fell out."

Savage snapped his fingers. "That's right. Zeb said Rosalie had brought Walter back into the fold. What if Axle arranged to meet Walter out at the quarry. He'd stolen Rosalie's motorcycle for transport, and he'd need someone to help him get out of Dodge. What if Walter didn't want to help him? They argued, shots were fired, Walter hit Axle in the chest."

"Twice," Lucas added.

Sinclair stayed silent, processing.

Savage gave a quick nod. "Have we checked those bullets against Walter's gun?"

Thorpe hesitated. "We don't have it. He was registered for a Glock 19, but unless we find it, that doesn't help much."

"Sinclair, arrange a search of his residence. You're looking for anything—a 9 mil, unregistered or not."

"If we're going with the theory that Walter shot Axle, then who killed Walter?" Sinclair stared at Savage. "Rosalie?"

There was a short silence. Savage knew they were thinking back to the horrific crime scene. The trailer sprayed with arterial blood. The puddle under Walter's body.

Sinclair's voice dropped to a whisper. "Would she really have slashed his throat like that?"

Thorpe swung away from his computer to glance Savage. "You know her best, boss. What do you think?"

Lucas didn't move, but his gaze was locked on Savage too.

He stared at the whiteboard cluttered with names and arrows, the ones now crossed out in red. A muscle worked in his jaw. "I don't want to think she's capable of something like that, but..." He shrugged. "We don't have another theory that fits."

"We can't even interrogate any of the suspects," Sinclair murmured. "Since they're all dead."

Lucas let out a sharp breath, almost a laugh.

"Then we have no way of proving any of it," Thorpe groaned, dropping his head into his hands.

Dammit.

Pressure throbbed behind Savage's eyes. He pinched the bridge of his nose and looked up. "We didn't check Rosalie's alibi for the night of Walter's murder." They'd been too distracted by Honey's disappearance, the wildfires, and the serious lack of sleep. Still, he should have followed up on that.

"You want me to pay her a visit?" Sinclair raised her eyebrows.

He shook his head. "I'll handle her. You search Walter's place. If we can put that one theory to bed, that would be something, at least."

She nodded, picked up her keys, and swung her jacket over her shoulder.

"I'll chase up on the autopsy and forensic reports on Walter's murder," Thorpe said, as Sinclair made for the door. They weren't the only ones who'd been distracted. Ray and Pearl had had their hands full treating evacuees. "There might be something there."

"Okay, good. I'll get Rosalie's alibi." He hoped to hell she had one. "On the way, I'll call the DEA and get an update on the Roadhouse. Now Beckett's in custody, it shouldn't be too hard to get them to back off."

"Rosalie will be pleased," Thorpe smirked.

"That's the idea." It would give him some leverage.

"What do you want me to do?" Lucas asked, straightening up.

A slow smile spread over Savage's face. "You have the honor of booking the councilor. Charge him with money laundering, conspiracy to commit murder, attempted kidnapping, and obstruction of justice—and anything else you can think of."

Lucas grinned as he got to his feet. "Happy to."

DUST DEVIL

SINCLAIR STEPPED out of the Sheriff's office and into a hot breeze. Her thoughts turned to Mason, and she couldn't stop herself from glancing at the mountains surrounding the town. They were charred but, as far as she could tell, not alight.

Still, she fired off a text message asking him if everything was okay. These were ideal conditions for a flare up, and the evacuees had only just returned to their homes. A massive clean-up operation was underway, with church groups, charities and volunteers offering to help rebuild and furnish damaged properties.

Maybe she'd look in on him later, once she'd searched Walter Minstrel's house. Trust her to fall for a fire chief. She snorted as she climbed into the cruiser. On the list of dangerous jobs, his was right up there.

That's why she understood how Becca felt about Savage. Loving a man like that was hard. Savage wasn't the type to take a backseat, always throwing himself into the thick of it in order to get his man. It was one of the things she admired about him. That endless search for justice, even at the expense of his relationship. A true lawman.

Walter Minstrel lived in a small, ranch-style house with peeling paint and a sagging porch roof. She wrinkled her nose as she got out of the car. He hadn't done much to keep the place up.

The gutters overflowed with dry leaves, and the grass hadn't been mowed in weeks. A beat-up truck rusted in the driveway, the hood propped open as if it were waiting for someone to come back and fix it.

Then again, the neighborhood was a patchwork of forgotten homes, chain-link fences, and barking dogs. Not exactly derelict, but close.

She noted it wasn't far from the Hidden Gem trailer park. Maybe three blocks, if you cut through the scrub. A two-mile ride from the Roadhouse. Everything within easy reach.

Sinclair used the keys recovered from Walter's body to let herself in. She didn't need a warrant, since Minstrel was dead. His home was now part of an active investigation tied to two homicides.

"Phew," she muttered, deciding to leave the front door open for some air. Inside was no better. The carpet was threadbare with unidentifiable stains on it, the furniture was old and outdated, and a dirty coffee cup and overflowing ashtray sat on the coffee table.

She pulled on gloves and then started her search in the living room. She lifted cushions, peered under furniture and behind vents, but didn't find anything. Only more cigarette butts and a pile of out-of-date porn mags.

The kitchen was the source of the foul odor. Unwashed dishes, empty pill bottles, fast food wrappers. Walter hadn't kept a healthy lifestyle. He was lucky he'd made it to forty.

She moved on.

Judging by his home and living conditions, Walter had led a simple life. The club must have meant everything to him. He'd been unmarried, struggling financially, and as far as she could see, didn't have much going for him other than Rosalie and the gang. No wonder he'd chosen to return to the fold rather than follow Axle into the unknown.

Sinclair was hit by a pang of melancholy.

In the back bedroom, things got more interesting. On top of the dresser, she found a half-empty box of 9mm Luger rounds. She stared at them, heart kicking up a beat.

Holding her breath, she opened the top drawer. Inside, tucked beneath a folded T-shirt, was a black Taurus semi-automatic pistol. 9mm. The same caliber that had put two holes in Axle Weston's chest.

Exhaling softly, Sinclair checked the slide. It was loaded, with one in the chamber. She ejected the magazine and counted the rounds. Six remained. It could have held more.

After bagging it, she inspected the drawer for additional ammunition or casing residue but didn't find anything. The rest of the search didn't yield anything more, so she stepped outside, re-locked the door behind her, and called Savage.

"Yeah?" came the familiar growl.

"I found Walter's sidearm. It's a nine mil. Taurus. It's also loaded. I'll drop it at Ray and Pearl's now, have them run ballistics."

"Nice work." He kept his tone level. They both knew better than to get their hopes up. A 9mm was the most common caliber out there, and odds were this one was registered to Walter Minstrel. They wouldn't know until they got the report whether it was the gun that killed Axle.

But it was something. And right now, something was better than nothing.

THIRTY-FIVE

SAVAGE ARRIVED at the hiking trail parking lot. Rosalie was already waiting when he pulled in. He saw her illuminated in his headlights, leaning against her black motorcycle, hair blowing in the warm breeze.

He'd sent her a message, and she'd responded with the coordinates. Honey and Ben were still at his house, and her place was risky, so they'd settled on somewhere in between the two of them.

"This better be good," she said as he stepped out of the Suburban. "I left a mighty fine BBQ to come see you."

"Shouldn't take long," he said, walking over to her.

She waited, hands on her hips, bathed in his headlights. It struck him she'd swapped her trademark leather pants for jeans and an olive-green shirt that made her eyes appear witchier than usual.

"I've got good news," he said, joining her in the SUV's beams. Rosalie stood around 5'7", but even in heeled boots, he had a good six inches on her. Not that she ever let that put her at a disadvantage.

She leaned forward, attentive, yet guarded. "What news?"

"I got the DEA to back off."

Her face lit up, and for a moment he saw how much the place

208

meant to her. How much it all meant. "Seriously? How the hell did you manage that?"

"Took Beckett into custody," he said, breaking into a grin. "Once he was out of the picture, the DEA lost momentum. They didn't want to be tied up in a corruption scandal, so they bailed."

Her voice hardened. "So Beckett was behind the raid?"

"Yeah. He'd been laundering drug money for Axle and didn't want it coming out. Diesel was the runner. He passed over the cash and Beckett cleaned it. Turned out they'd been skimming, only giving part of it to the club."

Her eyes widened. "That bastard. I swear I didn't know."

He believed her.

Rosalie looked away from him. "He kept a lot from me towards the end."

A flicker of something passed through her eyes. Not sadness. Frustration, maybe. Regret? But it only lasted a second and then her walls went right back up.

"I gathered."

She exhaled, then said, "Thank you, Dalton. I mean it. Guess I owe you."

Exactly what he'd been hoping for.

"Just doing my job. I know those drugs were planted. I won't tolerate corruption on my watch."

"How very noble of you." Her tone held a bite, but the corners of her mouth twitched. "So... is that it?"

He hesitated just long enough to cause her to stiffen.

"That's not it, is it?"

"No, I came here to ask you something, Rosalie. I feel like we know each other well enough now, so I'm not going to beat around the bush."

Her gaze narrowed. "I wouldn't say that, but I appreciate your directness. What do you want to know?"

"Did you kill Walter Minstrel?"

A short, incredulous laugh burst out of her. "Seriously? I leave a barbecue for this? You get the Feds off my back and now you're accusing me of murder?"

He didn't rise. "You're the only real suspect I've got. Walter betrayed the club. You had motive."

She shook her head. "You don't give up, do you?"

"No, ma'am."

She rested her hands on her hips. "Tell me, Dalton. Do you always get your man?"

"Or woman. Yes, generally speaking."

"And you think this was me? You think I slashed Walter's throat and left him to bleed out in the arms of a drugged-up hooker?" At his sharp look, she nodded. "Oh, yeah. I heard what happened. News like that gets around."

He frowned. "Did you do it?"

"For fuck's sake. Of course not. Why would I kill Walt? He turned his back on Axle. Swore loyalty to me and the club. There was no reason to get rid of him. Especially like that. That's crazy."

"Maybe you wanted to make an example out of him?"

She leaned toward him. "Even if I wanted to kill him, I wouldn't do it like that. Too messy. Besides, it would bring too much heat on the club."

He tried to get a read on her, but as usual, he failed. If she was lying, she deserved a goddamn Oscar. "Maybe that's what you want me to think."

She chuckled. "Come on, Dalton. What do you take me for?"

He had to admit, he didn't think it was her style. She was more sophisticated than that. "Okay, just give me an alibi, and I'll take you off the list."

She shrugged. "I was where I always am, at the Roadhouse. Joel helped me lock up around three."

He tilted his head back. "I'm going to need to verify that."

She rolled her eyes. "I'll send the camera footage over."

"Appreciate it."

"You know, I could take offense, but I won't because you got my bar back."

He smirked. "Glad to hear it. One more thing…"

She threw her hands in the air. "Jesus, Dalton."

"Hold your horses. I want to run something by you—off the record."

Her brows arched. "Does this implicate me or the club?"

"Not directly."

She sighed. "All right. Off the record. Shoot."

"Could Walter have shot Axle out at the quarry?"

"Walter? Shit. Why would he do that? He and Axle went way back."

Savage frowned. "It's all supposition at this point, but Axle could have asked for his help, and Walter refused. You said yourself, he'd pledged loyalty to the club. To you."

She stared at him. "You think they argued?"

"Axle would've been pissed. It could have escalated. If Axle threatened him, would Walter have shot him?"

A long beat passed while she considered this.

"I guess anything's possible," she said. "Walt wasn't the sharpest tool in the box, but he did have a temper. Shooting Axle—?" She shook her head. "Nah. I just don't see it."

Savage had to admit, it was a stretch.

"Okay, thanks. I'll let you get back to your BBQ now."

"It's probably gone cold," she grumbled. "But as long as you're happy."

He walked back toward the Suburban. "I will be once you send me that footage." In the tinted reflection of the window, he saw when she flipped him the middle finger.

He couldn't resist a grin as he got behind the wheel. She was one of a kind, all right.

There was a deep-throated growl as she started the Harley's engine, and a moment later, Rosalie roared past him and out of the lot.

"SHE WAS AT THE ROADHOUSE, like she said," Thorpe told Savage when he got to the office the next morning.

As promised, Rosalie had sent through the bar's surveillance footage from the night of Walter's murder, and Thorpe—always the early bird—had spent the better part of the last two hours trawling through it.

"Yes, but was she in the bar, or in her office?"

"Both. I took down the timestamps."

Savage went over. "Yeah?"

"She was in her office from 9:00 to 10:30, then again from 12:37 to about 1:20. At 1:21AM she walks into the bar and talks to Scooter for an hour. They're sitting right in front of the camera."

"What was time of death again?" Sinclair asked, coming over to join them.

"After 1:00 AM," Savage muttered. "Tonya's statement says she was with Walter until one, when she fell asleep. He was still alive at that point."

"She *could* have done it before she walked into the bar," Sinclair pointed out. "It only takes about fifteen minutes to get from the Hidden Gem back to the Roadhouse. It's on the same road."

Savage nodded to Thorpe's screen. "Show me?"

Thorpe swiveled around. A few moments later, he'd brought up the relevant video and forwarded to 1:21AM. "There. See?"

They watched as Rosalie opened the door from her office and walked into the bar. She looked around, greeted a few people, then sat next to Scooter at the bar.

"Does that look like someone who's just slashed a man's throat?" Savage murmured.

They all peered at the image of Rosalie. Calm, composed, poised —head bent, talking to her VP, a glass of bourbon on the bar in front of her.

"No," Sinclair stated, spinning around from the screen and

walking back to her desk. "I don't like Rosalie, but it doesn't. She's too relaxed. There's no way that woman could've just committed an act of extreme violence. Besides, wouldn't she have blood all over her?"

"She would've had to change," Savage agreed. "And there was no time."

"Unless I'm mistaken, those are the exact same clothes as earlier," Thorpe pointed out, studying the still playing video footage.

Sinclair nodded from her chair. "They are. I recognize the black, off-the-shoulder top."

"So that's that, then." Savage shoved his hands into his pockets. "She's in the clear. Unless..."

They all turned to him.

"I wonder... is it possible to alter the timestamp?"

Thorpe took off his glasses and cleaned them on his shirt. "Sure, it's possible. The footage could have been tampered with. But to avoid detection, they'd need some pretty sharp video editing skills, and I'm pretty sure no one in the Crimson Angels has that."

Savage frowned. He'd reviewed the member profiles himself. "You're right. Nobody's got that level of tech expertise. And anyway, that would take time. I asked Rosalie for the footage last night, and she sent it through this morning."

"In my opinion, it's legit," Thorpe confirmed.

Savage sucked in a deep breath, then let it out slow. "We can cross her off the list. She didn't do it."

There were murmurs of agreement from Thorpe and Sinclair.

Then, on the footage, Rosalie leaned over and picked up her bourbon—with her left hand.

THIRTY-SIX

SAVAGE BLINKED. "WAIT. REWIND THAT."

They studied it again, a heavy silence settling over the bullpen.

Lucas walked in, took one look at their faces and stopped. "What's up?"

Sinclair just shook her head. "It won't hold up."

Lucas glanced between them. "What won't hold up?"

They showed him the footage. He stood behind Thorpe's desk and watched right up until the end, then his eyebrows shot up. "She's left-handed."

"Circumstantial," Thorpe said, brushing it off.

"Coincidence?" Lucas looked at Savage, who shrugged.

"Maybe." But he was worried. How had he never noticed Rosalie was left-handed before? Had she been playing him this whole time?

"What do you want to do, boss?" Lucas asked, taking off his jacket and throwing it over his chair. He perched on the edge of his desk, arms crossed.

"Nothing we can do. A half-decent defense attorney will tear us apart. They'll subpoena every left-handed person within ten miles of

214

the trailer park." He nodded at the frozen image on the screen. "That, in itself, means nothing."

Sinclair pursed her lips. "We could search her place. Do a trash pull. Hit the curb outside her house and check around the vicinity. Maybe she stashed the weapon or bloody clothes nearby."

Lucas nodded, but Savage was already shaking his head. "Not without probable cause—and we don't have it. The only eyewitness was out cold, we haven't found the murder weapon, and there is no trace evidence linking Rosalie to the scene. Without something concrete, no judge in this county will sign off on a search warrant."

Sinclair scowled. "So we're just going to let it go?"

"For now, yeah." Savage arched his back, ironing out the kinks. A bad feeling gnawed at his gut. "Unless something new turns up, we've got nothing that'll stick."

Had Rosalie been toying with him? Cooperating just enough to earn his protection, while carrying out her own form of justice behind his back? Could she really have slipped out the bar's back door in the early hours, gone to the Hidden Gem trailer park, crept inside Tonya's trailer, and slashed Walter Minstrel's throat?

Not out of rage, but as a macabre warning.

A message to anyone thinking about challenging her authority.

He shook his head. She was nothing if not ruthless. And he already knew how far she'd go to stay in control.

"EVEN IF SHE CHANGED HER CLOTHES," he muttered, more to himself now, "she had time to dump them. The DEA tore that place apart. Anything incriminating would've been long gone before they stepped through the front door."

Sinclair exhaled but said nothing more.

Turning away from the recording, Savage went into his office and closed the door. Had he underestimated Rosalie Weston? Had their newfound truce skewed his judgement?

He sighed. Maybe he was reading too much into it. So what? She

L.T. RYAN

was left-handed. A lot of people were. It could be a coincidence, nothing more.

Part of him didn't believe she was capable of something so brutal.

Or maybe he just didn't want to.

THE DAY DID NOT IMPROVE. Pearl called just after lunch with the ballistics report from the Taurus semi-automatic pistol and bullets Sinclair had found in Walter's house.

"*Not* a match to those used to shoot Axle Weston," she told him.

"Dammit."

So much for that theory.

"Sorry to disappoint," she continued, "but that gun did not kill your dead biker."

He thanked Pearl, then strode out of his office to tell the others. They were all working, heads down, eyes glued to their computers. "If Walter did it, he didn't use that gun."

Sinclair glanced up. "I didn't find any evidence of a second weapon, legal or otherwise."

"Guess we were wrong," Thorpe mused. "It wasn't him."

Another dead end.

When were they ever going to catch a break? Honey and Ben were still at his place, even though the missing persons alert had been cancelled. Sure, Beckett and his thugs were behind bars, but neither Diesel, Axle nor Walter's killer had been found, and Savage didn't feel it was safe to let them come out of hiding just yet.

Or maybe he was just paranoid. Scarred by experience. The last time he'd dropped his guard, Becca and Connor had been abducted.

Shit. He rubbed his eyes, still gritty from too little sleep. This case had him tied up in knots. They all felt it. Something had to give soon.

He was about to leave for the day when his cellphone beeped. Glancing down, he saw it was Zeb.

216

DUST DEVIL

"This is Savage." He held the phone to his ear as he crossed the street to the Suburban.

"Can you come over?" Zeb sounded strange.

He paused. "Sure, what's up?"

"It's best if we talk here."

"On my way."

He arrived to find Zeb waiting out front, vaping. That was new. He was usually a pack a day kind of guy. Always had been as long as Savage had known him.

The former cop nodded when he saw him. "Thanks for coming."

Savage frowned. "Something wrong?"

"There's something—or rather, someone—you're going to want to see. Follow me."

Unsure where this was going, Savage followed Zeb inside his mobile home. His gut told him this was important, and deep down, Zeb was a cop at heart. He still liked to play the hero when the occasion presented itself, even though he'd long since left law enforcement behind.

Savage walked in and froze. Standing in the living room was a nymph of a woman. Five foot, if that, slender, and fragile-looking. She had soft, wavy hair and a wide mouth, although it wasn't smiling.

Zeb gestured to her. "This is Noel."

For a moment, Savage went blank, then he remembered. "The same Noel who used to work here?"

Who'd taken Zeb's gun and claimed it had been stolen.

Zeb nodded. "She came looking for work, but I told her I don't have capacity."

Noel's thin arms were wrapped around her tiny frame, almost as if she was hugging herself. "I've been working checkout at a convenience store in Santa Fe, but they accused me of stealing and fired me. I swear, I didn't take anything. I wouldn't do that."

Except she'd taken Zeb's gun.

Savage met Zeb's gaze. It was bright, knowing, and he got it. Zeb

217

didn't want her going back to the life, not after she'd managed to get out. By refusing her a job, he was giving her a chance.

"I asked Noel if she remembered taking my gun." Zeb's gaze flickered back to the young woman. "She admitted it was for protection."

"I had this john," she explained, hugging herself tighter. "He used to knock the girls around, you know?"

Savage nodded. Unfortunately, he did. He'd seen the aftermath more than a few times.

"I knew Zeb had a gun in the house, so one night I borrowed it, just in case.

"You use it?" Savage asked.

She shook her head. "No, I didn't need to. I don't even know how to shoot a gun. I just wanted to frighten the guy, in case he got any ideas."

He nodded as Zeb looked on. "What happened to it?"

She bit her lip. "I stashed it under the mattress, but I forgot to return it. When I remembered a couple of days later, it was gone."

Savage glanced at Zeb, who gave a slight nod. "Noel's always been straight. I have no reason to doubt her."

"When was this?" Savage asked, trying to piece the timeline together.

Noel bit her lip, thinking. "Maybe three years ago."

Savage stared at her. "Did you know Honey Granger?"

Noel smiled for the first time since he'd walked in. "Yeah. She was nice. It was Honey who gave me the courage to leave, to go get a job. She said if she could do it, so could I."

"You stayed in touch after she left?" Savage asked, surprised.

"Not really. I knew she was giving up the life. She wanted to get clean, settle down, have a family. Honey always had ambitions. She made me think I could too."

The bad feeling that had been gnawing at him worsened. As much as he wished it away, it wouldn't budge.

"Was Honey working here the same time as you?"

"Yes, that's how we met."

DUST DEVIL

Zeb gave a stiff nod.

"The same time the gun went missing?"

Zeb's gaze clouded over. Noel looked alarmed. "What are you saying, Sheriff? That Honey took it? She wouldn't do that."

"I'm not saying anything." But his chest constricted, while his pulse kicked up a notch. He glanced at Zeb. "I have to go."

The former cop nodded.

Savage turned to Noel. "Thank you for talking with me."

"Oh, okay. Sure." Her gaze flicked to Zeb as if to say, *is that it?*

Savage strode toward the door, his mind racing. Suddenly, all the pieces slotted into place.

And not the way he wanted them to.

An afterthought pierced the whirling mental turmoil, and he turned back. "Noel, give Zeb your contact details. There's a diner in Durango that might be able to give you work. If you're interested, that is?"

She nodded eagerly.

Zeb gave a pleased nod.

Savage raised a hand, thanking him, then left. As he climbed into his Suburban, the tightness in his chest got worse, because he now knew who'd killed Axle—and why.

219

THIRTY-SEVEN

THE DRIVE to the farm took fifteen agonizing minutes. He wished it were longer.

Much longer.

Every mile brought him closer to something he didn't want to do. Something he still wasn't sure he could go through with. But the more he turned it over in his mind, the more it added up.

Honey Granger.

She'd been in the right place at the right time. She'd stolen the gun three years ago and held onto it. Maybe for protection. Maybe because she never trusted Axle Weston or his grip on Diesel. Even back then, she'd been prepared to take matters into her own hands. But she never got the chance.

When Diesel disappeared, she knew exactly what happened to him. One thing he'd learned about Honey Granger was that she was no fool. She knew her lover was dead. That she'd have to raise her child alone—and she wanted retribution.

But the fates had intervened. Maybe it was a blessing in disguise. Axle had been arrested and charged with life imprisonment. He was out of her reach.

DUST DEVIL

So she let it go. Or she buried it.

But Savage was willing to bet she'd listened to what was on that phone. She'd worked out that Diesel had been laundering money for the Crimson Angels, and that's why Axle wouldn't let him leave.

He shook his head. All that bullshit about finding the phone in a box in her mother's attic. Lies. All of it. And he'd fallen for it.

He'd believed her, but then why wouldn't he? She was a single mother, scraping by. Living with her mom. Trying to give her son a stable life.

He imagined how it must have played out. Then, she heard Axle Weston had escaped. Busted out of prison, helped by the MC she hated. She'd pulled the gun out of hiding and plotted her revenge. A chance to corner him. A chance to get justice.

Had she used the flip phone to send him a message? To meet her at the quarry? Had she pretended it had come from Rosalie, or one of his biker buddies?

Then she'd gone to confront him.

No, to kill him.

To exact her revenge. For Diesel. For what she'd lost. For everything Axle had taken.

Shit!

The whole thing was premeditated, and there was no way she could argue otherwise. Not with the evidence stacked against her.

Savage pulled up outside his house and killed the engine. He sat in the dark, staring at the front door, his hands frozen on the wheel.

Axle had been a piece of work. No question about that. But nobody had the right to be judge, jury, and executioner. No matter what injustices they'd suffered.

Not even Honey.

He forced himself out of the truck. The porch light was on. The windows glowed softly. Inside, she was probably reading to Ben. He pictured the boy playing with Connor's old fire truck, and something twisted deep in his chest.

It wasn't fair. She'd suffered enough. She got justice—her way.

But now he'd have to tear that child's world apart again. Leave him without a mother. Put her behind bars.

"Stupid girl," he muttered, climbing the steps.

But he understood vengeance. He remembered what he'd felt when Axle had run Becca off the road. She'd been pregnant at the time. Defenseless. The bastard had left her for dead in a ditch until Savage had found her. She'd been bruised, bleeding. It was a miracle they hadn't lost the baby.

He clenched his jaw and slid the key into the lock.

Inside, the house was still. Music played softly from the spare room, a gentle acoustic guitar, almost mournful. There were two plates drying by the sink. She'd made dinner and washed up after them.

"Honey?" he called, his voice low.

He moved down the hall, toward the room at the end. His heart pounded harder the closer he got.

"Honey," he said again, knocking gently. "Can we talk?"

The door was shut, but the music pulsed quietly behind it.

He waited. No answer.

"I'm coming in."

He turned the handle.

The room was spotless. The bed was made. Toys neatly packed away. A handwritten note lay on the pillow—but Honey and Ben were gone.

SAVAGE STEPPED into the sheriff's office just after eight o'clock, sunglasses still on, a cup of coffee in hand. Barb wasn't in yet, neither was Sinclair, but Thorpe was at his desk, tapping away on his computer. Lucas sat quietly, studying police reports.

"Morning," Savage said, his voice rough.

"Morning." Thorpe looked up. "I've been going through CCTV footage, but there's no sign of Rosalie heading to the Hidden Gem the night Walter Minstrel was murdered."

DUST DEVIL

"She wouldn't have taken her motorcycle," Savage said. "Too loud. People would notice. She'd have used her truck or borrowed a vehicle."

"Couldn't see her truck either," he added. "I'm now looking for any vehicle belonging to club members."

He nodded. "Keep me posted."

Savage moved to his office and set the coffee down without sipping it. He felt like shit. As much as he'd tried, sleep hadn't come. He couldn't get Honey out of his mind. Her note had been short, but polite. She'd thanked him for helping her and Ben, but it was time to move on. That was it. No mention of anything else, but then she was too smart to incriminate herself by putting that in writing.

Lucas, as intuitive as ever, followed him in. "Everything all right?"

Savage ran a hand down his jaw. The stubble felt thicker than usual. He hadn't shaved. He hadn't done much of anything.

"I woke up this morning," he muttered, "and Honey and Ben were gone."

His deputy frowned. "Gone? You think it's suspicious?"

He shook his head. "No, nothing like that. She made the bed, took the kid, and vanished. Left a Thank You note, though."

Thorpe came to join them. "She didn't say goodbye in person?"

"Nope."

Lucas frowned. "So she just walked out in the middle of the night?"

"Yep."

"And you don't think that's strange?"

Savage shrugged. "Not particularly. She's been through a lot. I imagine she wanted some space. Maybe goodbyes aren't her thing."

Thorpe shrugged, while Lucas narrowed his gaze. "Should we call her mother, just to be safe?"

Savage shook his head. "Nah. Now that Beckett's behind bars and Axle's dead, she'll be fine." He couldn't meet their eyes when he said it.

223

Sinclair came in, saw them clustered in the doorway, and joined them. "What's going on?"

"Honey's disappeared," Thorpe said.

"She left," Savage corrected. "Of her own volition."

Sinclair shrugged. "Don't suppose it matters."

Savage felt Lucas's eyes on him, but the newest deputy didn't say anything.

"Let's tie off this investigation," Savage decided. "There's no point in keeping it open any longer."

Thorpe adjusted his glasses. "What's our theory? That Axle killed Diesel because he couldn't afford to let him leave the club?"

"Or he didn't want him telling anyone about the skimming. They were making a lot of money that the club never knew about."

Thorpe nodded. "I'll write it up."

"What about Axle?" Lucas asked.

Savage met his gaze. "I guess we'll never know who killed him. Could have been Walter, and that's why someone slit his throat."

"Rosalie?" Sinclair asked.

He shrugged. "Or one of the other Angels. Impossible to prove without evidence."

"To be continued..." Lucas said softly.

Savage gave a little nod. "So it seems."

Thankfully, they let it go.

Thorpe and Sinclair returned to their desks. Lucas lingered another second, then left, too.

That was the end of it.

But Savage didn't sit down. He stood by the window, hands braced on the sill, staring out at Main Street like it might deliver an answer. He hadn't told his team about the note. He hadn't mentioned that he'd stood outside her empty bedroom for twenty minutes, the note still folded in his hand. That he'd driven around for an hour before sunrise, not really looking, not ready to find her. That he'd considered calling it in. Hell, his thumb had hovered over Thorpe's number twice.

DUST DEVIL

But he hadn't done it.

Savage gave a heavy sigh. He was the sheriff of Hawk's Landing. He'd brought in Becca, his own fiancée, for interrogation when she'd withheld information in a murder case. He'd stood by while the justice system steamrolled people he cared about because that was the job. The law was the line. It had to be.

So why had he crossed it now?

He raked a hand through his hair, uneasiness eating him up inside. Because he knew why.

Because Honey Granger wasn't a threat.

Because Axle Weston had it coming.

Because a mother taking revenge for the man she loved and the life she'd lost didn't seem like a crime—just a tragedy.

Because a boy needed his mother.

Turning away from the window, he crossed the room and dropped into his chair.

Except, she'd killed a man.

But then, Axle had killed Diesel.

Was justice still justice if it happened outside the law?

He fingered his badge. It may as well have been burning a hole in his chest. What was it worth if he could set it aside when it suited him?

He'd upheld the law his whole life, at the expense of sleep, of happiness, of his relationship with Becca.

Becca.

He'd called her last night, desperate to talk. In one of life's brutal ironies, she hadn't answered. What would she say if she knew? Would she be disappointed in him? Relieved he was human? Would she be angry?

You wouldn't bend the rules for me, but you did for this woman? A stranger.

Would she say what he feared?

You let a murderer go.

He stared down at his desk, unable to shake off the weight of his decision. There was still time to act. Honey wouldn't have gotten far, not with a kid in tow. He could still catch her, bring her back. Get her to confess.

Still, he didn't move.

What good would it do?

All he'd achieve would be to leave a kid without his mother. There was no risk of her killing again, not now Axle was dead. She couldn't go home, couldn't use her real name. She'd forever be on the run, always looking over her shoulder, wondering if he was coming for her. Wasn't that punishment enough?

He reached for a report on his desk. Opened it but didn't read.

The gnawing doubt remained. Was this who he was now? A man who bent the rules for the right people.

And if he was, how did that make him any better than Zeb, or Jeffries, or Beckett, for that matter?

His predecessor's words came back to haunt him.

You're stuck in the same web of lies I was. You can't win this one, Boy Scout.

THIRTY-EIGHT

THE PARKING LOT at Devil's Bluff was nearly empty. A handful of vehicles stood parked beneath the fading light, their owners still somewhere up in the ridge trails, watching the sunset or maybe just not ready to come down yet.

The wildfires were finally out.

Ash clung to the edges of the road like old snow, and the hills above Hawk's Landing wore a mantle of blackened earth. Smoke no longer hung in the air, but the scent of it lingered in the dust, in the charred pine, in everything. The town had been spared, mostly. A few homes lost, land destroyed, but no lives. Not this time.

The vegetation would grow back. Eventually.

Savage stood beside his Suburban, arms folded across his chest, eyes on the horizon. The sky had turned to copper, then bruised into purple. The wind had stilled. All that remained was the hush of pending darkness.

He heard the soft purr of a motorcycle before he saw it. Then, from the bend in the road, she appeared.

Rosalie.

The motorcycle rolled to a stop beside him, and she climbed off,

L.T. RYAN

her boots kicking up a scatter of gravel. She tugged off her helmet and let her hair fall loose around her shoulders.

Once again, she'd forgone her traditional leather for denim jeans and a soft gray T-shirt. Her face, stripped of its usual armor of liner and shadow, looked different in the dying light. Calmer. Softer. There was a kind of serenity in her now, a contentment he hadn't seen before. It struck him that she looked... happy. Beautiful, even.

Savage found himself wondering how someone like that could have so savagely, so deliberately, slit a man's throat.

She walked over, not quite smiling. Not quite frowning either. "You wanted to see me?"

He nodded once. "Yeah, thanks for coming."

A pause stretched between them like a wire.

"I know it was you, Rosalie," he said, low, measured.

Her eyes didn't flicker. "You'll have to be more specific."

It wasn't denial so much as a test. A cautious probe of ground neither of them had stepped on before. He watched her closely, weighing the ease in her posture against the tension in her jaw.

"Walter," he said simply.

Another beat.

Her brow arched slightly, then she looked away toward the mountains. The fire-scarred ridges caught the last light, glowing faintly like cooling embers. "That wasn't me."

He gave a soft snort. "Nobody else had motive."

A soft sigh. "Neither did I." She turned back to him. "I'm not the monster you think I am."

He didn't reply.

"You solve Axle's murder?" she asked, tone easy but sharp around the edges.

"Nope," he said. "Guess we'll never know who shot him."

Rosalie narrowed her eyes, just a fraction. "That okay with you? From what I remember, you always get your man."

It was disturbing how well she was getting to know him, whereas he was beginning to feel like he didn't know her at all.

228

DUST DEVIL

"Not this time."

After a brief moment, she nodded. "What's happening with Beckett?"

"He's going to trial."

"Hope you get an unbiased judge." Rosalie knew as well as he did the repercussions of messing with the Guardians.

"He tried to kill us. No way he's going to get away with that." There was a pause. "Thanks for your help with that, by the way."

She smirked. "Always happy to see justice served."

Now that was ironic.

"That it?" she asked, her head tilted toward the setting sun. The soft, golden glow accentuated the green in her eyes.

"For now," he said.

She smiled. "It's been a pleasure, as always. You take care of yourself, Dalton."

"You too, Rosalie."

———

THE MAYOR WAS WAITING when Savage stepped into the office the next morning.

As always, McAllister was dressed like an oil baron running for re-election—dark suit, fitted waistcoat, starched collar, and a Stetson that caught the morning light. His boots gleamed. So did the sheen of perspiration on his flushed face.

"Sorry to hear about Beckett," he said as Savage ushered him inside and closed the door. "Terrible, terrible thing. I had no idea."

Sure you didn't, Savage thought, watching him sweat. Beckett's ties to the Crimson Angels were going to sting for a while—and not just in the press. McAllister had backed him more than once. Now, the stink clung to everything.

"Who's taking over?" Savage asked.

"One of his aides. Smart lady. Ivy grad. Name's Nancy Monroe."

That sounded promising. "About my funding—"

229

"I'll chase up," the mayor cut in quickly. "Beckett approved it. Should go through soon."

Savage nodded, managing a smile. "Good to hear."

McAllister shifted on his feet. "Read your report on the biker deaths. See you drew a line under that mess."

"Seemed prudent," Savage said. "Can't prove much with Diesel, Walter, and Axle all dead."

"Probably some club business gone bad," McAllister offered. "That's why Beckett wanted them shut down."

Savage held his gaze. "Is it?"

The mayor didn't answer. Just tipped his hat. "Well, Sheriff, I just wanted to say: well done. I'm sorry for the mess. There won't be any room for corruption in Hawk's Landing going forward."

"Glad to hear it."

They shook hands. As the door closed behind him, the office felt quieter than it should. Lucas sat at his desk, sorting reports. Barb was just hanging up the phone.

"Go home, Dalton," she said, stepping out from behind the counter. "Lucas and I have it covered. You need a break."

He hesitated. Without Becca and Connor, his house was full of memories. And regrets.

"Go see your family," Barb added gently, resting a hand on his arm.

The longing that hit him was swift and sharp. Not just for Connor's laugh or Becca's quiet steadiness—but for the life he'd started building before everything fractured.

Lucas looked up and gave him a nod. "She's right. We've got this." The deputy was more than capable, Savage knew that.

"Okay," he said. "I think I will."

Barb smiled. "Enjoy it. And bring them home."

He nodded, heading for the door.

The case was closed. The fire was out. But inside him, something still smoldered—guilt, maybe, or hope. Hard to tell the difference these days.

DUST DEVIL

Either way, he was going to try. Try to convince Becca that despite everything, he could still be the man she believed in. That they could still be a family.

He wasn't sure if it was too late.

But some things were worth chasing.

Even after the smoke had cleared.

The story continues in Savage Season. Grab your copy today!
https://a.co/d/74MaCk5

Join the L.T. Ryan reader family & receive a free copy of the Rachel Hatch story, *Fractured*. Click the link below to get started:
https://ltryan.com/rachel-hatch-newsletter-signup-1

Join the L.T. Ryan private reader's group on Facebook here:
https://www.facebook.com/groups/1727449564174357

THE DALTON SAVAGE SERIES

Savage Grounds

Scorched Earth

Cold Sky

The Frost Killer

Crimson Moon

Dust Devil

Savage Season

Join the L.T. Ryan reader family & receive a free copy of the Rachel Hatch story, *Fractured*. Click the link below to get started:

https://ltryan.com/rachel-hatch-newsletter-signup-1

ALSO BY L.T. RYAN

Find All of L.T. Ryan's Books on Amazon Today!

The Jack Noble Series
The Recruit (free)

The First Deception (Prequel 1)

Noble Beginnings

A Deadly Distance

Ripple Effect (Bear Logan)

Thin Line

Noble Intentions

When Dead in Greece

Noble Retribution

Noble Betrayal

Never Go Home

Beyond Betrayal (Clarissa Abbot)

Noble Judgment

Never Cry Mercy

Deadline

End Game

Noble Ultimatum

Noble Legend

Noble Revenge

Never Look Back

Bear Logan Series

Ripple Effect

Blowback

Take Down

Deep State

Bear & Mandy Logan Series

Close to Home

Under the Surface

The Last Stop

Over the Edge

Between the Lies

Caught in the Web

The Marked Daughter (Coming Soon)

Rachel Hatch Series

Drift

Downburst

Fever Burn

Smoke Signal

Firewalk

Whitewater

Aftershock

Whirlwind

Tsunami

Fastrope

Sidewinder

Redaction

Mirage

Faultline (Coming Soon)

Mitch Tanner Series

The Depth of Darkness

Into The Darkness

Deliver Us From Darkness

Cassie Quinn Series

Path of Bones

Whisper of Bones

Symphony of Bones

Etched in Shadow

Concealed in Shadow

Betrayed in Shadow

Born from Ashes

Return to Ashes

Risen from Ashes

Into the Light (Coming Soon)

Blake Brier Series

Unmasked

Unleashed

Uncharted

Drawpoint

Contrail

Detachment

Clear

Quarry

Dalton Savage Series

Savage Grounds

Scorched Earth

Cold Sky

The Frost Killer

Crimson Moon

Dust Devil

Savage Season

Maddie Castle Series

The Handler

Tracking Justice

Hunting Grounds

Vanished Trails

Smoldering Lies

Field of Bones

Beneath the Grove

Disappearing Act (Coming Soon)

Affliction Z Series

Affliction Z: Patient Zero

Affliction Z: Abandoned Hope

Affliction Z: Descended in Blood

Affliction Z : Fractured Part 1

Affliction Z: Fractured Part 2 (Coming Soon)

Alex Hayes Series

Trial By Fire (Prequel)

Fractured Verdict

11th Hour Witness

Buried Testimony

The Bishop's Recusal (Coming Soon)

Stella LaRosa Series

Black Rose

Red Ink

Black Gold

White Lies

Silver Bullet (Coming Soon)

Avril Dahl Series

Cold Reckoning

Cold Legacy

Cold Mercy (Coming Soon)

Savannah Shadows Series

Echoes of Guilt

The Silence Before

Dead Air (Coming Soon)

————

Receive a free copy of *The Recruit*. Visit:

https://ltryan.com/jack-noble-newsletter-signup-1

ABOUT THE AUTHOR

L.T. RYAN is a *Wall Street Journal, USA Today*, and Amazon best-selling author of several mysteries and thrillers, including the *Wall Street Journal* bestselling Jack Noble and Rachel Hatch series. With over eight million books sold, when he's not penning his next adventure, L.T. enjoys traveling, hiking, riding his Peloton,, and spending time with his wife, daughter and four dogs at their home in central Virginia.

* Sign up for his newsletter to hear the latest goings on and receive some free content ➜ https://ltryan.com/jack-noble-newsletter-signup-1
* Join LT's private readers' group ➜ https://www.facebook.com/groups/1727449564174357
* Follow on Instagram ➜ @ltryanauthor
* Visit the website ➜ https://ltryan.com
* Send an email ➜ contact@ltryan.com
* Find on Goodreads ➜ http://www.goodreads.com/author/show/6151659.L_T_Ryan

———

BIBA PEARCE is a British crime writer and author of the Kenzie Gilmore, Dalton Savage and DCI Rob Miller series.

Biba grew up in post-apartheid Southern Africa. As a child, she lived on the wild eastern coast and explored the sub-tropical forests and surfed in shark-infested waters.

Now a full-time writer, Biba lives in leafy Surrey and when she isn't writing, can be found walking through the countryside or kayaking on the river Thames.

Visit her at bibapearce.com and join her mailing list to be notified about new releases, updates and special subscriber-only deals.

Printed in Dunstable, United Kingdom